艾瑪

Emma

原著 _ Jane Austen
改寫 _ Elspeth Rawstron
譯者 _ 王傳明

ABOUT THIS BOOK

For the Student

🎧 Listen to the story and do some activities on your Audio CD.

📺 Talk about the story.

⭐ Prepare for Cambridge English: Preliminary (PET) for schools.

For the Teacher

HELBLING e·ZONE THE EDUCATIONAL PLATFORM A state-of-the-art interactive learning environment with 1000s of free online self-correcting activities for your chosen readers.

Go to our Readers Resource site for information on using readers and downloadable Resource Sheets, photocopiable Worksheets, and Tapescripts. www.helblingreaders.com

For lots of great ideas on using Graded Readers consult Reading Matters, the Teacher's Guide to using Helbling Readers.

Level 4 Structures

Sequencing of future tenses	Could / was able to / managed to
Present perfect plus yet, already, just	Had to / didn't have to
First conditional	Shall / could for offers
Present and past passive	May / can / could for permission Might for future possibility
How long?	Make and let
Very / really / quite	Causative have Want / ask / tell someone to do something

Structures from lower levels are also included.

CONTENTS

ABOUT THE AUTHOR

Jane Austen was born in December 1775. She had seven brothers and sisters, and she was the second youngest in the family. The Austens lived in Steventon in Hampshire, where their father was a vicar[1]. They were a happy, well-educated[2] and affectionate[3] family.

Jane Austen began to write stories for her family when she was twelve years old. When she was a teenager, she really wanted to be an author. In all her novels, Jane Austen writes about marriage, but she never married herself. She fell in love with[4] Tom Lefroy, a young law student, but he later married the sister of another student. An old friend Harris Bigg-Wither asked her to marry him. But she did not love him and she did not accept his proposal[5]. As she

wrote in a letter to her niece, Fanny, "the worst[6] thing you can do, is marry somebody you don't love." This was an unusual[7] view[8]. To most women in the 1800s love was not as important as wealth[9] or a good position[10] in society[11].

Jane Austen wrote her six great novels in a very short time. *Sense and Sensibility* in 1811; *Pride and Prejudice* in 1813; *Mansfield Park* in 1814; *Emma* in 1814–15; *Northanger Abbey* and *Persuasion* were published[12] in 1817 after her death. They were all published anonymously[13], but in her lifetime[14] people discovered that she was the author. The Prince Regent[15] was a fan[16] of her novels and he wanted her to dedicate[17] *Emma* to him.

In 1816, Jane Austen became ill. She died in Winchester in July 1817 and is buried in Winchester Cathedral.

1 vicar [ˈvɪkɚ] (n.) (英國國教) 教區牧師
2 well-educated [ˌwɛlˈɛdʒuketɪd] (a.) 有教養的
3 affectionate [əˈfɛkʃənɪt] (a.) 溫柔親切的
4 fall in love with sb 和某人談戀愛
5 proposal [prəˈpozḷ] (n.) 求婚
6 worst [wɜst] (a.) 最差的
7 unusual [ʌnˈjuʒʊəl] (a.) 不尋常的
8 view [vju] (n.) 觀點
9 wealth [wɛlθ] (n.) 財富
10 position [pəˈzɪʃən] (n.) 地位
11 society [səˈsaɪətɪ] (n.) 社會
12 publish [ˈpʌblɪʃ] (v.) 出版
13 anonymously [əˈnɑnəməslɪ] (adv.) 不具名地
14 lifetime [ˈlaɪfˌtaɪm] (n.) 一生
15 Prince Regent 攝政王 (即後來的喬治四世)
16 fan [fæn] (n.) 狂熱愛好者；迷
17 dedicate [ˈdɛdəˌket] (v.) 題獻 (著作)

Jane Austen began writing *Emma* in January 1814 and she finished it in March 1815. *Emma* was then published in December 1815 by John Murray, who also published the works of the poet Lord Byron. The novel was published in three volumes[1].

Jane Austen famously advised[2] her niece that, three or four families in a country village are the perfect subject[3] for a novel, and this is exactly what she wrote about. *Emma* is set in the small village of Highbury in the south of England, and it follows the relationships[4] of a small group of people in the village: Emma and Mr Knightley, Frank Churchill and Jane Fairfax and their friends and families.

1 volume [ˋvɑljəm] (n.) 卷；冊
2 advise [ədˋvaɪz] (v.) 勸告；忠告
3 subject [ˋsʌbdʒɪkt] (n.) 主題
4 relationship [rɪˋleʃən͵ʃɪp] (n.) 關係
5 aim [em] (n.) 目標
6 character [ˋkærɪktɚ] (n.) 角色
7 duty [ˋdjutɪ] (n.) 義務；職責
8 social order 社會秩序
9 break the rule 打破規則
10 result [rɪˋzʌlt] (n.) 結果
11 fit into 融入
12 community [kəˋmjunətɪ] (n.) 社區
13 polite [pəˋlaɪt] (a.) 禮貌的
14 equal [ˋikwəl] (a.) 相等的
15 rely on . . . 依靠……
16 imagination [ɪ͵mædʒəˋneʃən] (n.) 想像力

At that time, a young woman's aim[5] was to marry as well as she could. The main character[6], Emma, decides not to marry. This is unusual. It's a woman's duty[7] to marry. But because Emma is rich, she doesn't have to marry.

The moral theme in *Emma*, is that there is a social order[8]. If the characters break the rules[9] of their society, the result[10] is illness or unhappiness. People must be honest about their relationships. If they are not, they'll be unhappy. To be happy you must fit into[11] the community[12] you live in, and you must be polite[13] and kind to everybody in that community. We're told in the novel that true love and a good marriage can only happen if you choose someone of an equal[14] position in society, equal education and equal good looks.

Emma thinks that several of the characters are in love with each other, but she is always wrong. She relies on[15] her imagination[16]. She sees love as it is in the romantic novels of the time, which Jane Austen disliked.

1 Which of these were true in Jane Austen's time (1775–1817)? Tick (✓) true (T) or false (F).

T F [a] A woman could ask a man to marry her.

T F [b] A woman couldn't ask a man to dance.

T F [c] A man and a woman couldn't go for a walk together.

T F [d] When a father died, he couldn't leave his house to his daughter.

T F [e] An educated woman could be a teacher.

2 What could help you to find a husband in Jane Austen's time? Tick (✓).

_____ [a] having a university degree

_____ [b] being wealthy

_____ [c] being able to play the piano well

_____ [d] having a good job

_____ [e] being beautiful

_____ [f] being able to paint and draw well

3 These novels show daily life at the time they were written. Have you read any of them? Tick (✓).

4 Match the events in *Emma* with the pictures.

1. going to a ball
2. having tea
3. going for a picnic
4. having a dinner party

5 Look at the pictures in Exercise **4**. Guess which character is Emma. In pairs ask and answer questions about the pictures.

a) Which event do you think is part of Emma's daily life?

b) Which event do you think is a special occasion?

c) What is Emma doing in each picture?

6 Match the words with their definitions.

_____ a match-making   1 being connected to somebody and having feelings for them

_____ b marriage

_____ c engagement   2 the man you marry

_____ d wife   3 formal promise to marry somebody

_____ e relationship   4 trying to find somebody a good partner

_____ f husband   5 the woman you marry

6 legal union between a man and a woman

7 These verbs are from the story. Match them to their meanings.

——— a miss
——— b chat
——— c criticize
——— d flatter
——— e be keen
——— f expect
——— g agree
——— h be glad
——— i admire
——— j blush

1 talk
2 be happy
3 say yes
4 feel sad when someone isn't with you
5 talk about somebody's bad points
6 want to do something very much
7 say nice things about somebody
8 think somebody is wonderful
9 go red with embarrassment
10 think something will happen

8 Write the adjective forms of these nouns.

a embarrassment ⬛⬛ b ⬛ r ⬛⬛⬛⬛⬛ ed

b vanity ⬛⬛ i ⬛

c misery ⬛⬛⬛ er ⬛ bl ⬛

d kindness ⬛⬛⬛ d

e nervousness ⬛⬛ rv ⬛⬛ s

f excitement ⬛ x ⬛⬛⬛ ed

a Before an important meeting.

b When someone shouts your name across a room of people.

c When someone you like doesn't like you.

10 Complete the sentences with the adjectives in Exercise **8**.

a Everybody was _____ and happy about going for a picnic.

b Frank Churchill went all the way to London to have his hair cut. Emma thought this was very _____ behavior.

c It was very _____ of the person to buy Jane a piano.

d Mr Woodhouse felt _____ when his wife died.

e Emma was angry with herself and _____ for being so cruel to Miss Bates.

f Mrs Weston didn't know Frank very well. She was _____ about his visit.

11 Listen to the descriptions of the characters and number the pictures.

a

Mr Knightley

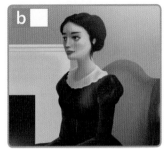

b

Jane Fairfax

c

Emma Woodhouse

d

Mr Woodhouse

e

Frank Churchill

f

Mr Weston

Chapter 1

Emma Woodhouse was happy, beautiful, clever and rich. At twenty-one, there was nothing in her life that upset[1] her. She was the youngest daughter of a very affectionate father, Mr Woodhouse. Her elder sister, Isabella, was married and lived in London, and her father was widowed[2], so Emma was the mistress[3] of his house.

Emma's mother died when she was five, and Emma and Isabella were brought up[4] by Miss Taylor, a very kind and loving[5] governess[6]. Miss Taylor loved both daughters, but particularly[7] Emma. They lived together as friends and Emma did whatever she wanted.

Unhappiness came at last[8] when Miss Taylor married. The marriage to Mr Weston was a happy one, and Emma really liked Miss Taylor's husband. But now she felt miserable[9]. She had no friends at home, and she missed Miss Taylor very much.

Emma's father hated change, and marriage brought change. On the evening after Miss Taylor's wedding day[10], they sat together and Emma smiled and chatted[11] as cheerfully[12] as she could.

---

1 upset [ʌpˋsɛt] (v.) 使心煩；使不適
　（三態：upset; upset; upset）
2 widowed [ˋwɪdod] (a.) 喪偶的
3 mistress [ˋmɪstrɪs] (n.) 女主人
4 bring up 養育長大
5 loving [ˋlʌvɪŋ] (a.) 慈愛的
6 governess [ˋgʌvənɪs]
　(n.) 家庭女教師

7 particularly [pəˋtɪkjələlɪ] (adv.) 特別地
8 at last 最後；終於
9 miserable [ˋmɪzərəbl̩]
　(a.) 不幸的；悽慘的
10 wedding day 婚禮日
11 chat [tʃæt] (v.) 聊天；閒談
12 cheerfully [ˋtʃɪrfəlɪ] (adv.) 興高采烈地

But when tea came, Mr Woodhouse said, "Poor Miss Taylor! I wish she was here. What a pity[1] that Mr Weston wanted to marry her!"

"I can't agree with you," said Emma. "Miss Taylor couldn't live with us forever, and now she has a house of her own."

"A house of her own! But why does she need a house of her own? This house is three times[2] as large."

"We'll go and see them often, and they'll come to see us," Emma promised.

Emma wanted to cheer her father up[3], so she decided to play a game of backgammon[4]. But just as she prepared the backgammon table, a visitor walked in. It was Mr Knightley, a good-looking man, of about thirty-seven. He was a very good friend of the family, and he was the elder[5] brother of Isabella's husband. He lived about a mile away from Hartfield, and he often visited them. Mr Woodhouse was very pleased[6] to see him.

"I hope the wedding went well," said Mr Knightley. "Who cried most?"

"Ah! Poor Miss Taylor!" said Mr Woodhouse.

"Poor Mr and Miss Woodhouse," said Mr Knightley, "not poor Miss Taylor. It must be better to have only one husband to look after[7] instead of you two."

"Especially when *one* of those two is very difficult!" said Emma joking[8]. "That's what you mean."

"That's very true," said Mr Woodhouse. "I'm afraid I am sometimes very difficult."

"Father, I didn't mean *you*. I meant myself. Mr Knightley loves to criticize[9] me."

Mr Knightley was one of the few people who could see faults[10] in Emma Woodhouse, and the only person who ever told her about them.

"Emma knows I never flatter[11] her," said Mr Knightley.

"Emma," said her father, "will really miss Miss Taylor."

"Of course Emma will miss her," said Mr Knightley. "But all Miss Taylor's friends must be glad[12] that she is so happily married."

---

1 what a pity 好可惜

2 time [taɪm] (n.) 倍

3 cheer up 使高興起來

4 backgammon [ˌbæk'gæmən] (n.) 西洋雙陸棋戲

5 elder ['ɛldɚ] (a.) 較年長的

6 pleased [plizd] (a.) 高興的；喜歡的

7 look after 照顧

8 joke [dʒok] (v.) 開玩笑

9 criticize ['krɪtɪ,saɪz] (v.) 批評

10 fault [fɔlt] (n.) 錯誤；過失

11 flatter ['flætɚ] (v.) 奉承

12 glad [glæd] (a.) 高興的

"And you've forgotten," said Emma, "that I made the match[1] myself."

Mr Knightley shook[2] his head at her.

Her father said, "Please don't do any more match-making[3], Emma."

"I promise I won't do it for myself, but I will for other people. It's great fun! And now I've been successful, I can't stop match-making."

"I don't understand what you mean by 'successful'," said Mr Knightley. "People can find themselves a husband or wife."

"Please don't make any more matches," said Mr Woodhouse.

"Only one more. I must find a wife for Mr Elton."

"If you want to be kind to Mr Elton, ask him to dinner."

"Yes," said Mr Knightley, laughing. "Invite him to dinner, Emma, but leave him to choose his own wife. A man of twenty-six can find his own wife."

Match-making

- Do you think match-making is positive[4] or negative[5]?
- Have you ever tried match-making your friends?

---

1 match [mætʃ] (n.) 婚配
2 shake [ʃek] (v.) 搖（三態：shake; shook; shaken）
3 match-making [ˈmætʃˌmekɪŋ] (n.) 作媒
4 positive [ˈpɑzətɪv] (a.) 正面的
5 negative [ˈnɛgətɪv] (a.) 負面的
6 first wife 第一任妻子
7 offer [ˈɔfɚ] (v.) 提供
8 be dying to 極度想……
9 belong to 屬於……
10 intend [ɪnˈtɛnd] (v.) 想要；打算

Mr Weston's first wife[6] was from a very rich Yorkshire family, the Churchills. She died three years after their marriage, and she left a son, Frank. Frank's aunt and uncle, Mr and Mrs Churchill didn't have any children, so they offered[7] to look after him, and they all lived together at Enscombe in Scotland.

The next twenty years of Mr Weston's life passed happily. He bought Randalls, a large house near the village of Highbury in the south of England, which he loved. He saw his son once a year, and he was very proud of him. Highbury felt very proud of Frank Churchill, too, and everyone was dying to[8] meet him. A visit was often talked about but never happened.

Now, although Emma wasn't interested in marrying, she often thought that she should marry Frank Churchill. He seemed to belong to[9] her. She thought that all their family and friends must want them to get married. And she was sure that Mr and Mrs Weston wanted them to marry. She really wanted to meet him. And she intended[10] to like him, and to be liked by him.

On Emma's next visit to Randalls, she heard some exciting news.

"Frank is coming to stay," said Mr Weston, showing her into the sitting room. "I had a letter from him this morning."

"That's wonderful news!" said Emma. "And Mrs Weston must be happy, too."

"Yes, but she doesn't think that he'll come."

Emma spoke to Mrs Weston about it. "His visit depends on[1] his aunt agreeing to it," she said. "Mrs Churchill is jealous[2] of his love for his father."

Mr Frank Churchill didn't come. A letter of apology[3] arrived. He was very sorry that he couldn't come, but Mrs Churchill needed him at home. Mr and Mrs Weston were very disappointed[4], and Emma told Mr Knightley of their disappointment.

"I'm sure he could come if he wanted to," said Mr Knightley.

"I don't know why you say that. He really wants to come, but his uncle and aunt won't let him."

"If Frank Churchill really wanted to see his father, he could arrange[5] it. A man of his age. What is he? Twenty-three or twenty-four."

"That's easily said by you."

"He's got money, and he's got free time. We know that he's got a lot of both. We're always hearing about him being at some seaside[6] resort[7] or other. A little while ago, he was at Weymouth. That proves[8] that he can leave the Churchills."

"Yes, sometimes he can."

"There's one thing, Emma, which a man can always do, and that's his duty. It's Frank Churchill's duty to visit his father. He should say to Mrs Churchill—I must go and see my father. He'll be hurt[9] if I don't visit him."

Frank Churchill

- Who is Frank? Tick (✓) the correct boxes.
  - ☐ Mr Weston's son by his first marriage.
  - ☐ Miss Taylor's son.
  - ☐ Mr and Mrs Churchill's nephew.
  - ☐ The Churchill's son.

(9)

"Mr Frank Churchill couldn't talk like that to his uncle and aunt."

"Then he's a very weak[10] young man," said Mr Knightley.

"I'm sure he isn't a weak young man," cried Emma. "You seem determined[11] to think badly of him."

"Me! Not at all," replied Mr Knightley. "I'd like to sing his praises[12], but I haven't heard anything good about him, except that he's tall and good-looking. Oh, and he's polite."

"Then, he'll be very popular in Highbury. We don't see many tall, good-looking young men here. If he visits, there'll be only one subject in Donwell and Highbury—Mr Frank Churchill."

1 depend on 視……而定
2 jealous [ˋdʒɛləs] (a.) 妒忌的
3 apology [əˋpɑlədʒɪ] (n.) 道歉
4 disappointed [ˌdɪsəˋpɔɪntɪd] (a.) 失望的；沮喪的
5 arrange [əˋrendʒ] (v.) 安排
6 seaside [ˋsiˌsaɪd] (a.) 海邊的
7 resort [rɪˋzɔrt] (n.) 度假名勝
8 prove [pruv] (v.) 證明
9 hurt [hɝt] (v.) 傷害；受傷 (三態：hurt; hurt; hurt)
10 weak [wik] (a.) 弱的
11 determined [dɪˋtɝmɪnd] (a.) 堅決的
12 sing somebody's praises 大為讚嘆

🎧 10

"If I find him intelligent[1], I'll be glad to make friends with him. But if he is only a good-looking chatterbox[2], I won't spend any time with him."

"I think he's one of those people who can get on with[3] everybody," said Emma. "Everybody will like him. He'll talk to you about farming, to me about drawing or music, and so on[4] to everybody. That's my idea of him."

"And mine," said Mr Knightley, "is, that if he's anything like that, he'll be awful[5]!"

"I won't talk about him any more," cried Emma. "We're both prejudiced[6]. You against him, and I for him."

"Prejudiced! I'm not prejudiced. I don't think about him at all," said Mr Knightley.

Emma couldn't understand why he was angry. It wasn't like Mr Knightley to dislike somebody without meeting them.

1 intelligent [ɪnˈtɛlədʒənt] (a.) 有才智的
2 chatterbox [ˈtʃætɚˌbɑks] (n.) 喋喋不休的人
3 get on with sb 與某人關係良好
4 and so on 等等；諸如此類
5 awful [ˈɔfʊl] (a.) 極糟的
6 prejudice [ˈprɛdʒədɪs] (v.) 使抱有偏見
7 apologize [əˈpɑləˌdʒaɪz] (v.) 道歉
8 wonder [ˈwʌndɚ] (v.) 想知道
9 escape [əˈskep] (v.) 逃脫
10 throw [θro] (v.) 丟；扔
（三態：throw; threw; thrown）
11 tremble [ˈtrɛmbl̩] (v.) 顫抖

Chapter 3

The next day, Emma was in the village of Highbury, so she decided to visit Mrs and Miss Bates. They loved to have visitors, and Mr Knightley was always telling her she should visit them more often.

And so that morning, Emma sat with them for an hour. The conversation, as always, soon turned to Jane Fairfax, their niece.

"We had a letter from Jane this morning," said Miss Bates.

Emma was polite, "I hope she's well."

"Yes, she's very well," replied Miss Bates, while looking for the letter. "Oh! Here it is. But, first of all, I really must apologize[7]. It's such a short letter—only two pages."

Emma wondered[8] if she could escape[9].

"It's two years, you know, since Jane was here," said Miss Bates.

"Is Jane coming to stay?"

"Oh yes, next week."

"That's good news," said Emma.

"Yes, it is. She's coming for three months. Colonel and Mrs Campbell are going to Ireland to stay with their daughter, Mrs Dixon, and her husband. Mr Dixon's a lovely young man. You know, he saved Jane's life at Weymouth. They were in a boat, and she was nearly thrown[10] into the sea. I tremble[11] when I think of it! But ever since we heard about that, I've been very fond of Mr Dixon! And so Jane is coming here next Friday or Saturday. I'm so excited! Well, now let's read her letter. I'm sure she tells her own story much better than I can."

"I'm afraid I must go," said Emma, quickly, not wanting to hear the contents[1] of the letter again. "My father's waiting for me at home. I must say goodbye now."

Jane Fairfax's parents died when she was a child, so she went to live with her grandmother and her aunt. Then, one of her father's friends changed her destiny[2]. That friend was Colonel Campbell.

When Jane was nine, she went to live with the Campbells. They had a daughter, Miss Campbell. She was about the same age as Jane, and they became good friends. Jane was lucky. She had an excellent[3] education there.

Then Miss Campbell fell in love with Mr Dixon, an eligible[4] young man, and they got married.

Jane was now twenty-one, and she wanted to work. She was qualified[5] to teach children. She was coming to Highbury to spend her last months of freedom[6] with her aunt and grandmother.

Highbury, instead of welcoming Mr Frank Churchill, must put up with[7] Jane Fairfax.

Emma was sorry to have to be polite to a person she didn't like for three long months! Why didn't she like Jane Fairfax? That was a difficult question to answer. Mr Knightley said it was because Emma wanted to be like Jane.

---

1 content [ˈkɑntɛnt] (n.) 內容
2 destiny [ˈdɛstənɪ] (n.) 命運
3 excellent [ˈɛkslənt] (a.) 出色的
4 eligible [ˈɛlɪdʒəbl] (a.) 合適的
5 qualified [ˈkwɑləˌfaɪd] (a.) 合格的；勝任的
6 freedom [ˈfridəm] (n.) 自由
7 put up with 忍受

She disagreed[1] with him at the time. But she knew this was true. There were other reasons as well. Jane was too cold and too shy[2]! Everybody made such a fuss of[3] her! And everybody thought they should be friends because they were the same age.

On the arrival[4] of Jane Fairfax, Emma paid a visit[5]. Jane Fairfax was tall and elegant[6]. Her hair was dark, and her skin was pale[7]. She had deep gray eyes, with dark eyelashes[8] and eyebrows[9]. She was more beautiful than Emma remembered.

During that first visit, Emma decided that she couldn't dislike Jane any longer. And she was sorry that there weren't any eligible young men in Highbury for Jane to marry—nobody that she could match-make her with.

But these feelings didn't last[10]. Jane spent an evening at Hartfield with her grandmother and her aunt. That evening, Jane never gave her real opinion[11] about anything. In particular, she was very secretive[12] on the subject of Weymouth and the Dixons.

Emma decided that Jane was hiding something. Maybe Mr Dixon was really in love with Jane. Perhaps he only chose to marry Miss Campbell because of her wealth.

1 disagree [ˌdɪsəˈgri] (v.) 不同意
2 shy [ʃaɪ] (a.) 害羞的；提防的
3 make a fuss of . . . 對……大驚小怪
4 arrival [əˈraɪvl̩] (n.) 到達
5 pay a visit 去拜訪
6 elegant [ˈɛləgənt] (a.) 雅緻的
7 pale [pel] (a.) 蒼白的
8 eyelash [ˈaɪˌlæʃ] (n.) 睫毛
9 eyebrow [ˈaɪˌbrau] (n.) 眉毛
10 last [læst] (v.) 持續
11 opinion [əˈpɪnjən] (n.) 意見
12 secretive [ˈsikrɪtɪv] (a.) 隱隱藏藏的

(14) 　　Jane was secretive about other topics, too. She and Mr Frank Churchill were at Weymouth at the same time. Emma knew they were a little acquainted[13], but Emma couldn't get a syllable[14] of information from Jane as to what he was like.

"Was he handsome?"

She believed people thought he was quite good-looking.

"Was he likeable?"

She believed everybody thought he was polite.

"Was he clever?"

She didn't know Mr Churchill well enough for her to comment[15].

Emma couldn't forgive her.

Secretive

- Could you be friends with someone who is very secretive?
- Is being secretive a good or a bad thing? Discuss in small groups.

13　acquainted [əˋkwentɪd] (a.) 認識的
14　syllable [ˋsɪləbl̩] (n.) 一言半語；少許表示
15　comment [ˋkɑmɛnt] (v.) 評論

Chapter 4

The next morning, Emma decided to visit the Westons.

"Good news!" said Mr Weston when she arrived. "Frank is coming tomorrow—I had a letter this morning—he'll be at Randalls by dinner-time."

Emma smiled, and she congratulated Mr Weston.

"I'll bring him to Hartfield tomorrow evening," he said.

"Oh, yes. Please do," said Emma.

"Think of me tomorrow, Emma, about four o'clock," said Mrs Weston, who was nervous about the visit.

"I will," said Emma, before she left to go home.

The morning of the interesting day arrived, and Emma remembered at ten, and eleven, and twelve o'clock, that she was to think of Mrs Weston at four.

At twelve o'clock, she opened the sitting room[1] door, and to her surprise, she saw two gentlemen sitting with her father— Mr Weston and his son.

"Frank arrived a day early," explained Mr Weston.

Frank Churchill was actually here. He was a *very* good-looking young man. He seemed friendly, and he had a good sense of humor[2]. Emma liked him immediately.

16 　Frank Churchill liked Randalls, loved the location[3], the walk to Highbury, Highbury itself, Hartfield still more.

He seemed keen[4] to get to know Emma, and he asked her lots of questions. Was it a large neighborhood? Did she ride? Were there any good walks? Balls[5]? Did they have balls?

Emma answered all these questions, and then Mr Churchill began to talk about Mrs Weston.

"She's made my father very happy," he said. "I can't thank her enough."

Frank Churchill knew how to please[6] and he definitely[7] wanted to please Emma.

He finished by saying, "I'm surprised how young and beautiful Mrs Weston is. I didn't expect[8] to find a pretty[9] young woman."

"Don't let her know that you've called her a pretty young woman," said Emma, laughing.

"Of course not," he replied. "No, when I speak to Mrs Weston, I know who I should praise[10]."

1　sitting room 起居室；客廳
2　sense of humor 幽默感
3　location [loˋkeʃən] (n.) 位置
4　keen [kin] (a.) 渴望的
5　ball [bɔl] (n.) 舞會

6　please [pliz] (v.) 取悅
7　definitely [ˋdɛfənɪtlɪ] (adv.) 清楚地
8　expect [ɪkˋspɛkt] (v.) 期待；預期
9　pretty [ˋprɪtɪ] (a.) 漂亮的
10　praise [prez] (v.) 稱讚

(17) "Does he also know that people expect us to fall in love," wondered Emma. She saw Mr Weston looking at them with a happy expression[1], and she knew he was listening to their conversation.

How to please

- Do you know how to please?
- Think of a time when you did something to please someone else. Tell a friend.

Soon Mr Weston stood up to leave. He must go. He had to go to Highbury. His son stood up too and said, "While you are in Highbury, I'll go and visit an acquaintance[2]. I know one of your neighbors, a lady staying in Highbury, a family of the name of Barnes, or Bates. Do you know anybody called Bates or Barnes?"

"Of course we do," cried Mr Weston. "Mrs Bates—we passed her house—I saw Miss Bates at the window. That's right, you know Miss Fairfax. I remember you met her at Weymouth. Of course, you should go and see her."

---

1 expression [ɪkˋsprɛʃən] (n.) 表情
2 acquaintance [əˋkwentəns] (n.) 認識但不是很熟的人

"I don't need to visit her this morning," said the young man. "I could go another day, but we met at Weymouth so . . . "

"Oh, go today. Don't put it off[1]," said his father.

"Miss Fairfax told me that she knew you," said Emma. "She's a very elegant young woman."

He agreed, but with so quiet a "Yes", that she was sure he didn't mean it[2].

Then the two men left. Emma was very pleased with this beginning to their friendship.

Miss Fairfax

- What is Miss Fairfax's first name? What does Emma think of her? Go back to pages 26-27 to check.

1 put off 拖延	4 ballroom [ˋbɔl͵rum] (n.) 跳舞的大廳
2 don't mean it 不是有意的	5 organize [ˋɔrgə͵naɪz] (v.) 組織；安排
3 stop at . . . 停留某處	6 opposite [ˋɑpəzɪt] (prep.) 在對面

Chapter 5

The next morning, Mr Frank Churchill visited again. This time, he came with Mrs Weston. Emma wasn't expecting them, so it was a lovely surprise. She wanted to see him again, and especially with Mrs Weston. And when she saw them together, she was happy. Mrs Weston's love and friendship were important to him.

They went for a walk into Highbury together, and on the way, they stopped at[3] the Crown Inn. Emma told Frank Churchill about the old ballroom[4]. He was immediately interested. He looked at the ballroom through the window.

"There should be balls here every fortnight," he said. "Miss Woodhouse, why haven't you organized[5] a ball here? We must have a ball."

They walked on, and they were now almost opposite[6] the Bates's house.

"Did you visit the Bates family?" Emma asked.

"Oh, yes!" he replied. "It was a very successful visit. I saw all three ladies."

"And how did Miss Fairfax look?" asked Emma.

"She looked ill, very ill. However, Miss Fairfax is very pale, so she always looks ill."

Emma disagreed, "She doesn't look ill. She's got very beautiful pale skin."

"I've heard many people say that but I prefer a healthy complexion[1]," he said.

"Did you often see Jane Fairfax in Weymouth?" asked Emma.

"Hasn't Miss Fairfax already answered this question?"

"No, she hasn't," said Emma. "But then, she's very secretive. She doesn't want to give any information about anybody."

"Very well then, here's the truth. I often met her in Weymouth. Now, tell me," he continued. "Have you ever heard Miss Fairfax play the piano[2]?"

"Ever heard her!" repeated Emma. "I've heard her every year of our lives. She plays very well."

"Do you think so?" he continued. "I thought she played well. I remember Mr Dixon always liked her to play the piano."

"How did Miss Campbell feel about that? Was she jealous?"

"I don't know. The three of them seemed to have a good friendship," he began. Then, he paused[3] and added, "However, it's impossible for me to say. You know her better than I do."

"We've known each other a long time, but we've never been good friends. I couldn't be friends with anyone so shy and secretive."

"I don't like secretive people either," said Frank Churchill. "I could never love somebody so shy and secretive."

---

1 complexion [kəm`plɛkʃən] (n.) 膚色
2 play the piano 彈鋼琴
3 pause [pɔz] (v.) 暫停

They got on so well[1], and they thought so alike[2], that Emma couldn't believe it was only her second meeting with Frank Churchill.

Unfortunately, Emma's very good opinion of Frank Churchill was spoilt[3] the next day, when she heard this news from Mrs Weston, "He's gone to London to have his hair cut[4]."

Emma thought that this was very vain[5] behavior. However, apart from[6] this, Emma still had a good opinion of him. She was quite happy for him to be in love with her, or to be very nearly in love with her. Of course, she wasn't in love with him—she didn't want to get married.

Emma's good opinion of him increased when Mr Weston told her that Frank liked her very much—thought her very beautiful. She decided that she mustn't be too critical[7] of him.

However, there was one person who didn't approve[8]—Mr Knightley. He was told about the haircut[9], and Emma heard him say, "Hmm! Just the silly man I thought him to be."

---

1 get on so well 相處甚佳
2 alike [əˋlaɪk] (adv.) 相像
3 spoil [spɔɪl] (v.) 破壞（三態：spoil; spoil/spoilt; spoil/spoilt）
4 have one's hair cut 剪頭髮
5 vain [ven] (a.) 愛虛榮的
6 apart from . . . 除了⋯⋯
7 critical [ˋkrɪtɪkl] (a.) 愛挑剔的
8 approve [əˋpruv] (v.) 贊成；同意
9 haircut [ˋhɛr͵kʌt] (n.) 理髮

Chapter 6

Frank Churchill came back from London with his hair cut. He laughed at himself, but he didn't seem at all ashamed[10] of it.

On Tuesday, Mr and Mrs Coles were having a dinner party.

"Oh, good! Another opportunity[11] to guess how Frank Churchill feels about me," thought Emma. "If he's very much in love with me, I'll have to be a little cold towards[12] him."

That Tuesday evening, Emma followed another carriage[13] to the house, and she was pleased to see that it was Mr Knightley's. Mr Knightley, in Emma's opinion, didn't use his carriage enough. He waited to help her out of her carriage.

"You should always travel like this," said Emma. "Like a gentleman."

He thanked her, "How lucky that we arrived at the same time! For now, you see that I, too, can be like a gentleman."

"Oh yes, and *now* I'll be very happy to walk into the same room with you," she said smiling.

"Silly girl!" was his reply.

---

10 ashamed [əˈʃemd] (a.) 難為情的
11 opportunity [ˌɑpəˈtjunətɪ] (n.) 機會
12 towards [təˈwɔrdz] (prep.) 向；朝
13 carriage [ˈkærɪdʒ] (n.) 馬車

Gentleman

- Do you think Mr Knightley is a gentleman?
  Why / why not? Tell a friend.

At dinner, Emma was seated next to[1] Frank Churchill. She gave him all her attention[2] until she heard Mrs Cole say something interesting about Jane.

"I went to see Miss Bates, this afternoon," said Mrs Cole. "And I saw a piano. It was delivered this morning, and Jane doesn't know who sent it. They decided it must be from Colonel Campbell. But Jane had a letter from the Campbells recently, and they didn't mention[3] a piano."

Everybody agreed it must be from Colonel Campbell.

Emma turned to Frank Churchill.

"Why are you smiling?" she asked.

"No, you first. Why are *you* smiling?"

"Me! I think it's strange that he's never sent her a piano before," said Emma.

"Perhaps Miss Fairfax has never stayed here for so long before," replied Frank Churchill.

---

1 next to 在⋯⋯的旁邊
2 attention [əˈtɛnʃən] (n.) 注意
3 mention [ˈmɛnʃən] (v.) 提及；說起

"You're thinking what I'm thinking," said Emma. "I know you are!"

"Maybe," said Frank Churchill. "Tell me what you're thinking."

"I think the piano's from Mr Dixon," said Emma.

"Mr Dixon—yes, it could be a present from Mr and Mrs Dixon. I told you the other day that he really admired[1] her performance."

"Yes," said Emma, "and that confirmed[2] an idea of mine. I think that after Mr Dixon asked Miss Campbell to marry him, he fell in love with Jane. I'm telling you my thoughts but you don't need to agree with me."

"You could be right. Mr Dixon definitely preferred Jane's music to her friend's."

"And then, he saved her life. Did you hear about that? There was a boat trip—an accident[3]—she was about to fall off the boat. He caught her."

"I know. I was there on the boat," said Frank Churchill.

"Were you really?"

"Yes, I was. It happened very quickly. We were all shocked. Mr Dixon was no more shocked than anybody else."

"I wasn't sure before," said Emma, "but the arrival of this piano proves it. Mr Dixon is in love with Jane."

"I agree with you, that the piano is an offering[4] of love," said Frank Churchill.

---

1 admire [əd`maɪr] (v.) 欣賞
2 confirm [kən`fɝm] (v.) 證實；確認
3 accident [`æksədənt] (n.) 意外；事故
4 offering [`ɔfərɪŋ] (n.) 供物；提供

After dinner the ladies went through to the sitting room first. The men joined[1] them shortly after.

Frank Churchill walked in first. After saying good evening to Miss Bates and her niece, he made his way directly to where Emma sat. She was his object[2], and everybody must see that.

"I've made a very sad discovery," said Frank Churchill. "I've been here a week tomorrow—that's half my time."

"Perhaps you're sorry now that you spent one whole day having your hair cut."

"No," he said, smiling, "I don't regret[3] that at all. I don't like seeing my friends, unless I'm fit to be seen[4]."

The rest of the gentlemen were now in the room, so Emma had to turn from Frank Churchill for a few minutes, and listen to Mr Cole. When Mr Cole moved away, Emma saw Frank Churchill staring across the room at Miss Fairfax.

"What's the matter?" asked Emma.

He jumped. "Thank you," he said. "I've been very rude[5], but really Miss Fairfax has done her hair in a very strange way. I can't take my eyes off[6] her. I must go and ask her whether it's an Irish[7] fashion[8]. Shall I? Yes, I will. And you'll see how she takes it—whether she blushes[9]."

He went immediately. Emma soon saw him standing in front of Miss Fairfax, and talking to her. But he was standing exactly in front of Jane, so Emma couldn't see anything.

Before he could return to his chair, it was taken by Mrs Weston.

"My dear Emma, I've been dying to[10] talk to you. Do you know how Miss Bates and her niece came here?"

"They walked, of course."

"No, they didn't. They came in Mr Knightley's carriage. I think he only brought the carriage for them."

"That's very possible," said Emma, "He's so generous and kind."

Mrs Weston smiled and said, "I think it's more than generosity[11]. In fact, I've made a match between Mr Knightley and Jane Fairfax. What do you say to that?"

"Mr Knightley and Jane Fairfax!" exclaimed[12] Emma. "Dear Mrs Weston, how could you think of such a thing? Mr Knightley can't marry. What about my nephew Henry? He's going to inherit[13] Donwell Abbey from Mr Knightley."

"My dear Emma, if Mr Knightley really wants to marry, you can't stop him because of your nephew Henry, a boy of six years old?"

---

1 join [dʒɔɪn] (v.) 加入
2 object [ˋɑbdʒɪkt] (n.) 對象
3 regret [rɪˋgrɛt] (v.) 後悔
4 fit to be seen 看起來體面
5 rude [rud] (a.) 粗魯的
6 can't take one's eyes off sb
　 無法不注視某人

7 Irish [ˋaɪrɪʃ] (a.) 愛爾蘭的
8 fashion [ˋfæʃən] (n.) 流行樣式
9 blush [blʌʃ] (v.) 臉紅
10 be dying to do sth 極渴望做某事
11 generosity [ˏdʒɛnəˋrɑsətɪ] (n.) 慷慨
12 exclaim [ɪkˋsklem] (v.) 呼喊；驚叫
13 inherit [ɪnˋhɛrɪt] (v.) 繼承

(28) "Yes, I can. I couldn't bear[1] Henry to lose his inheritance[2]. Mr Knightley marry! And Jane Fairfax, too. I can't think of anyone worse[3]!"

"She's always been a favorite of his, as you very well know[4]."

"He's not in love with Jane. My dear Mrs Weston, don't start match-making. You're very bad at it. Jane Fairfax mistress of Donwell Abbey! No! Mr Knightley couldn't do such a mad thing."

"He's wealthier than she is, and there's a little difference in their ages, but I can't see anything unsuitable[5]."

"But Mr Knightley doesn't want to marry. Why should he marry? He's happy by himself: with his farm and his sheep, and his library. And he's very fond of his brother's children. He doesn't need to marry, either to fill up his time or his heart."

Mr Knightley

- Why does Emma say that Mr Knightley does not need to marry? Do you think she is right? Discuss with a friend.

---

1 bear [bɛr] (v.) 忍受
　（三態：bear; bore; borne）
2 inheritance [ɪnˋhɛrɪtəns] (n.) 繼承
3 worse [wɜs] (a.) (adv.) 較差

4 very well know (= know very well)
　知道的很清楚
5 unsuitable [ʌnˋsutəbl̩] (a.) 不適合的

"My dear Emma, if he really loves Jane Fairfax . . . "

"Nonsense[1]! He doesn't love Jane Fairfax. I'm sure he doesn't."

"But I've heard him speak very highly of[2] Jane! The interest he takes in her—his anxiety[3] about her health! Such an admirer of her performance on the piano, and of her singing! I've heard him say that he could listen to her forever. Oh, and I think this piano, that somebody has sent to Jane Fairfax, maybe it's from Mr Knightley."

"Oh, I don't think so," said Emma. "Mr Knightley doesn't do anything mysteriously[4]."

"I'm sure it's from him. I noticed that he was silent when Mrs Cole told us about it at dinner."

They talked about it for a while longer, until Mr Cole came over to ask Miss Woodhouse to play the piano and she agreed.

Then Frank Churchill came to sing, so Emma gave her place to[5] Miss Fairfax, who played much better than she did.

"We sang together once or twice at Weymouth," Mr Churchill told the guests.

Emma sat at a little distance⁶ from the piano and listened. Then she noticed Mr Knightley listening very carefully, and she began to think again about Mrs Weston's suspicions⁷.

She still didn't want Mr Knightley to marry. "His brother, Mr John Knightley will be disappointed. My father will miss his daily visits. And I can't bear the idea of Jane Fairfax at Donwell Abbey. A Mrs Knightley! No! Mr Knightley must never marry."

Mr Knightley came and sat next to her. At first, they only talked about the performance. He praised Jane's performance, but that wasn't unusual. She spoke of his kindness in bringing the aunt and niece. He didn't want to talk about it. But that only showed he didn't want to discuss his kindness.

"This gift from the Campbells," she said, "this piano is a very kind gift."

"Yes," he replied, with no embarrassment⁸. "But why didn't they tell her about it? Surprises are silly things."

Emma was now very sure that the piano was not from Mr Knightley. But whether he was in love, was still in doubt⁹.

1 nonsense ['nɑnsɛns] (n.) 胡說
2 speak highly of sb 高度稱讚某人
3 anxiety [æŋ'zaɪətɪ] (n.) 擔心
4 mysteriously [mɪs'tɪrɪəslɪ] (adv.) 神祕兮兮地
5 give one's place to sb 把位置讓給某人
6 distance ['dɪstəns] (n.) 距離
7 suspicion [sə'spɪʃən] (n.) 懷疑
8 embarrassment [ɪm'bærəsmənt] (n.) 難堪
9 in doubt 不能肯定的；懷疑的

Guess

- Who is the piano from?
- Who is in love with who? If you don't know, read on to find out.

Towards the end of Jane's second song, her voice was a little hoarse[1].

"That's enough," said Mr Knightley, thinking aloud. "You've sung quite enough for one evening."

Another song, however, was soon asked for. And Frank Churchill was heard to say, "I think you could play this one easily."

Mr Knightley was angry. "That man," he said, "just wants to show off[2] his voice." And touching Miss Bates, who at that moment walked by. "Miss Bates, your niece will sing herself hoarse. Go, and stop them."

Miss Bates stopped the singing, but then somebody suggested[3] dancing and Frank Churchill came up to ask Emma to dance.

---

1 hoarse [hors] (a.) 嗓音沙啞的
2 show off 炫耀
3 suggest [sə`dʒɛst] (v.) 建議

While waiting for the dance to start, Emma looked to see what Mr Knightley was doing. He didn't usually dance. If he danced with Jane Fairfax now, it could mean he liked her. No. He was talking to Mrs Cole. Somebody else asked Jane to dance.

Emma was no longer worried for little Henry. His inheritance was safe. She enjoyed the dancing. Frank Churchill was a good dancer. Unfortunately, it was late and two dances were all that there was time for.

"It's just as well[1]," said Frank Churchill, as he walked with Emma to her carriage. "I didn't want to ask Miss Fairfax to dance. You're a much better dancer than she is."

---

1 It's just as well. 這樣很好。

Chapter 8

Before midday[1] the next day, Frank Churchill arrived at Hartfield. He entered[2] the room with a big smile on his face.

"Miss Woodhouse," he began, "We're going to have a ball at the Crown Inn."

"The Crown!"

"Yes, you have to agree to it. It was my father's idea and Mrs Weston agreed. I left them there and came to Hartfield to tell you. They want you to come and join them at the Crown. They want your opinion."

Emma was very happy. The two young people set off[3] together immediately for the Crown. Mr and Mrs Weston were very happy to see her there.

They looked round the rooms together. And before they left the Crown, Emma agreed to have the first two dances with Frank Churchill. As they left, she heard Mr Weston whisper to his wife, "Oh, good! He's asked her to dance, my dear!"

The next morning, Emma sat at breakfast and all her thoughts were of the ball. Soon after breakfast, Mr Knightley arrived. Emma told him about the ball, but he wasn't at all interested in it.

"It's a lot of trouble for a few hours of noisy entertainment[4]," he said. "Of course, I must go to it. But I'd rather[5] be at home."

(34) Jane Fairfax, however, was excited. "Oh, Miss Woodhouse," she said, "I hope nothing will happen to stop the ball. I'm so looking forward to[6] it."

So it was not to please Jane Fairfax that he'd prefer to stay at home. No! Emma was sure that Mrs Weston was mistaken[7]. Mr Knightley was not in love with Jane Fairfax.

Sadly, that evening, a letter arrived from Mr Churchill asking Frank to come home immediately. Mrs Churchill was ill. Frank must set off for Enscombe as soon as possible.

A note was sent to Emma from Mrs Weston. Frank Churchill was coming to Hartfield to say goodbye.

They couldn't have the ball, and Frank Churchill was leaving. It was too awful!

Emma was ready for Frank Churchill before he arrived.

For the first few minutes of the visit, he sat lost in thought[8].

"Now, we can't have the ball," said Emma.

"If I come back, we'll still have our ball," said Frank Churchill. "And don't forget our dance."

Emma smiled.

"I've had a wonderful two weeks! I wish I could stay longer," he said.

---

1 midday [ˈmɪdˌde] (n.) 正午；中午
2 enter [ˈɛntɚ] (v.) 進入
3 set off 動身
4 entertainment [ˌɛntɚˈtenmənt] (n.) 娛樂
5 would rather 寧願；較喜歡
6 look forward to 期待（後接名詞或動名詞）
7 mistaken [mɪˈstekən] (a.) 弄錯的；誤解的
8 lost in thought 陷入沉思

Stay longer

- Do you ever wish you could stay longer?
  Tick (✓) and tell a friend.
  - ☐ on holiday
  - ☐ at a party
  - ☐ at a friend's house
  - ☐ at school
  - ☐ in a Math lesson
  - ☐ in bed

(35) "But won't you visit your friends, Miss Fairfax and Miss Bates, before you leave?"

"I've already been to see them. I was passing the house, so I thought it was the right thing to do." He hesitated[1], got up, walked to a window. "Perhaps, Miss Woodhouse, I think you've probably guessed. I'm . . . "

Emma felt, he was about to say something, which she didn't want to hear. To stop him, she said, "I'm glad you visited Miss Fairfax and Miss Bates."

He was silent. Emma heard him take a deep breath[2]. She didn't want him to speak, and he knew that. "Oh, dear! He's more in love with me than I thought," she said to herself.

Luckily, his father walked in, and it was time to go. A very friendly shake of the hand, a sad "Goodbye," and the door shut on Frank Churchill.

He was gone, and Emma felt miserable. She liked seeing him every day. "The last two weeks have been great fun," she thought. "And he *almost* told me that he loved me. And now, I feel so unhappy, I think I must be a little in love with him."

1 hesitate [ˈhɛzəˌtet] (v.) 躊躇；猶豫
2 take a deep breath 深呼吸一口氣

Chapter 9

The next day, Emma was having tea with Mrs Weston and Mr Knightley when the conversation turned to Jane Fairfax.

"But why does she want to stay at the vicarage[1] with Mr Elton and his new wife?" Emma asked.

"It's better than always staying at home," said Mrs Weston.

"You're right, Mrs Weston," said Mr Knightley.

Mrs Weston gave Emma a meaningful glance[2].

After a few minutes silence, he said, "And another thing—I'm sure Mrs Elton has never had a friend like Jane Fairfax before."

"I know you think very highly of Jane Fairfax," said Emma.

"Yes," he replied, "everybody knows I think highly of her."

"And yet," said Emma, "perhaps, you aren't aware[3] yourself *how* highly."

"Oh! Are you there? But you're very behind[4]," said Mr Knightley. "Mr Cole asked me about my feelings for Jane Fairfax six weeks ago."

He stopped. Emma didn't know what to think.

---

1 vicarage [ˈvɪkərɪdʒ] (n.) 牧師住宅
2 glance [glæns] (n.) 一瞥
3 aware [əˈwɛr] (a.) 知道的；察覺的
4 behind [bɪˈhaɪnd] (adv.) 落後

Then he continued, "Anyway, I'm sure Miss Fairfax doesn't want to marry me and I'm very sure, I'll never ask her."

Emma was pleased, "You're very modest[1], Mr Knightley," she exclaimed.

He didn't seem to hear her. He was thoughtful[2] and said, "So you've decided that I should marry Jane Fairfax?"

"No, I haven't. I don't want you to marry Jane Fairfax or Jane anybody. You won't sit and chat with us when you're married."

Mr Knightley was thoughtful again. "No, Emma, I've never thought of Jane in that way," he said. And soon afterwards[3], "Jane Fairfax is a very lovely young woman but she's too shy for me."

Emma was very happy to hear that Jane had a fault. "Well," she said, "and you soon silenced[4] Mr Cole, I suppose?"

"Yes, of course. I told him he was mistaken. He apologized and said no more. No, I admire Jane Fairfax, and it's always nice to talk to her, but that's all."

"Well, Mrs Weston," said Emma after Mr Knightley left, "do you still think Mr Knightley wants to marry Jane Fairfax?"

"My dear Emma, he's so sure he's *not* in love with Jane, that I'm sure he *will* fall in love with her in the end."

---

1 modest [ˈmɑdɪst] (a.) 謙虛的
2 thoughtful [ˈθɔtfəl] (a.) 深思的
3 afterwards [ˈæftəwədz] (adv.) 後來
4 silence [ˈsaɪləns] (v.) 使沉默
5 delighted [dɪˈlaɪtɪd] (a.) 高興的
6 elderly [ˈɛldəlɪ] (a.) 上了年紀的
7 stomach [ˈstʌmək] (n.) 腹部

Chapter 10

[38] Emma was sitting with Mrs Weston one morning when Mr Weston brought in a letter. It was from Frank Churchill. He was coming to Highbury again.

They began to prepare for the ball at the Crown again, and everybody was very excited. Only a few days stood between the young people of Highbury and happiness.

Finally, it was the evening of the ball. Mr Frank Churchill led a very happy Emma onto the dance floor for the first dance. She was delighted[5] by the thought of so many hours of fun before her. She was upset, however, because Mr Knightley wasn't dancing. He should be dancing, not standing with the husbands and fathers! He looked so tall and handsome next to the short elderly[6] men with their round stomachs[7]. Everybody must think that! And, except for Frank Churchill, he was the handsomest man in the room.

Emma

- Why is Emma happy? Why is she upset? Imagine you are Emma and explain your feelings to a friend.

The ball continued pleasantly, and then Emma suddenly noticed that Mr Knightley was dancing with Harriet. "Just as I imagined," thought Emma happily. "He's a very good dancer."

Emma had no opportunity to speak to Mr Knightley till after dinner. But when they were all in the ballroom again, he came over to talk her.

"My dear Emma," he said, "do you think you perfectly understand the degree of friendship between Frank Churchill and Miss Fairfax?"

"Oh, yes, perfectly. Why do you ask?"

"Have you never thought that he liked her, or that she liked him?"

"Never!" she cried. "And how could it possibly come into your head?"

"I've recently seen signs[1] of a relationship[2] between them— certain secretive looks."

"Oh, very amusing[3]! There's no relationship between them, I assure[4] you."

Just then, Mr Weston asked everybody to start dancing again. "Come Miss Woodhouse, Miss Fairfax, what are you all doing? Come and dance."

"I'm ready," said Emma.

"Who are you going to dance with?" asked Mr Knightley.

She hesitated a moment, and then she replied, "With you, if you'll ask me."

"Will you dance?" said Mr Knightley, offering his hand.

"Yes," said Emma happily.

1 sign [saɪn] (n.) 跡象
2 relationship [rɪˋleʃənˏʃɪp] (n.) 戀愛關係
3 amusing [əˋmjuzɪŋ] (a.) 有趣的
4 assure [əˋʃʊr] (v.) 保證

Chapter 11

The next day, they all went on a trip to Box Hill. It wasn't a happy day. At first, Emma was bored. "I've never seen Frank Churchill so silent and so stupid," she thought. He looked without seeing, and he listened without knowing what she said.

When they all sat down, it was better, because Frank Churchill was more talkative[1], and he flattered Emma. To the people who looked on, they seemed to be flirting[2].

1 talkative [ˈtɔkətɪv] (a.) 多話的；健談的
2 flirt [flɜt] (v.) 調情

Emma liked the attention, but Mr Churchill was not winning her heart. In fact, she planned to match-make him with her friend, Harriet.

"You're being very flattering," said Emma to Frank Churchill. "But," lowering her voice, "nobody is speaking except us, and we can't talk nonsense for the entertainment of seven silent people."

"Let everybody on the Hill hear me praise you," he said. And then whispering, "What shall we do to make them talk? I know—Ladies and gentlemen, Miss Woodhouse orders me to say, that she wants you each to say something entertaining[1]. She only asks for one very clever thing, or two quite clever things, or three very boring things, and she promises to laugh at them all."

(42) "Oh, very well," exclaimed Miss Bates, "then I don't need to worry. Three very boring things. That will do for me."

Emma couldn't resist[2]. "Ah, but that may be difficult for you. You can only say *three* things."

Miss Bates didn't immediately understand. But, when she did, she was very upset.

"Ah! Yes, I see what she means." Then turning to Mr Knightley, "I'll try to hold my tongue[3]."

"I like your plan," cried Mr Weston. "I'll do my best. What about a riddle[4]?"

"No good, I'm afraid," answered his son.

"Oh, please let me hear it," said Emma.

"I don't think it's very clever," said Mr Weston. "But here it is. What two letters of the alphabet are perfection[5]?"

"I don't know," said Emma.

"Ah, you'll never guess. You," to Emma, "I'm certain, will never guess. I'll tell you. "M" and "A"—Em-ma. Do you understand?"

It wasn't very funny, but Emma liked it and so did Frank Churchill and Harriet. The rest of the party didn't seem to find it so funny.

---

1 entertaining [ˌɛntəˈtenɪŋ]
  (a.) 有趣的
2 resist [rɪˈzɪst] (v.) 抗拒

3 hold one's tongue 保持沉默
4 riddle [ˈrɪdl̩] (n.) 謎
5 perfection [pɚˈfɛkʃən] (n.) 完美

"This explains the sort of clever thing you want. Mr Weston's done very well, but he's ruined[1] it for everybody else," said Mr Knightley gravely[2]. "*Perfection* shouldn't have come so soon."

"Pass[3] us, if you please[4], Mr Churchill," said Mrs Elton.

"Shall we walk, Augusta?" said Mr Elton.

"Yes, please. I'm tired of sitting in one place for so long. Come on, Jane, take my other arm."

Jane said no, and the husband and wife walked off.

"Happy couple!" said Frank Churchill. "Very lucky, marrying as they did. They only knew each other for a few weeks in Bath! Very lucky! How many men have married after a short acquaintance, and regretted it for the rest of their lives! I hope somebody will choose my wife for me. Will you choose a wife for me, Emma? I'm sure I'll like anybody you choose. Find somebody for me and educate her."

"And make her like myself."

"If you can."

"Very well, I will. You shall have a lovely wife."

Jane looked upset. "Now," she said to her aunt, "shall we join Mrs Elton?"

"If you want to, my dear." They stood up and walked off, followed by Mr Knightley.

Only Mr Weston, his son, Emma and Harriet remained[5]. Frank Churchill's lively[6] mood[7] became almost unpleasant. Even Emma grew tired of flattery and laughter. When the carriages arrived to take them home, Emma was relieved[8].

While she was waiting for her carriage, Mr Knightley came to speak to her.

"Emma," he said, "how could you be so rude to Miss Bates?"

Emma remembered, and blushed, but tried to laugh it off[9]. "She probably didn't understand me."

"I assure you she did. She talked about it after. You behaved badly[10], Emma! This isn't pleasant[11], Emma. But I must, I will tell you the truth while I can. I'm your friend."

While they talked, they were walking towards the carriage. It was ready and, before she could speak again, he helped her in. She said nothing. She was angry with herself and embarrassed.

After getting into the carriage, she sat back for a moment. Then she wanted to say goodbye to him. She turned to look at him but it was just too late. He wasn't looking, and the horses were moving.

---

1 ruin [ˈruɪn] (v.) 毀壞
2 gravely [ˈgrevlɪ] (adv.) 嚴肅地
3 pass [pæs] (v.) 跳過
4 if you please 煩請；勞駕
5 remain [rɪˈmen] (v.) 逗留
6 lively [ˈlaɪvlɪ] (a.) 活潑的；輕快的
7 mood [mud] (n.) 心情
8 relieved [rɪˈlivd] (a.) 放心的
9 laugh off 用笑擺脫（困境等）
10 behave badly 行為不佳
11 pleasant [ˈplɛzn̩t] (a.) 令人愉快

How could she have been so cruel to Miss Bates! Emma felt the tears running down her cheeks almost all the way home.

Emma

- Do you think Emma behaved badly?
- Do you tell your friends if they are rude to other people?
- Should friends tell each other the truth? Discuss in small groups.

The horrible[1] trip to Box Hill was in Emma's thoughts all evening. She decided to go and see Miss Bates the next morning to apologize.

On her return to Hartfield, Emma found Mr Knightley and Harriet sitting with her father.

Mr Knightley immediately stood up. He looked very serious. "I wanted to see you before I left," he said. "I'm going to London, to spend a few days with John and Isabella. Have you anything to send or say?"

"Nothing at all," replied Emma. "But this is very sudden."

"Yes, it is."

"He hasn't forgiven me," thought Emma.

1 horrible [ˈhɑrəbl] (a.) 糟透的

Just as Mr Knightley was about to leave, her father asked, "How did you find my old friend and her daughter? Dear Emma has been to call on[1] Mrs and Miss Bates, Mr Knightley."

Emma blushed and looked at Mr Knightley. He smiled at her.

She was happy and a moment later even happier. Mr Knightley took her hand, and was about to kiss it—when, for some reason or other, he suddenly let it go[2].

"Why did he change his mind[3]? He shouldn't have stopped," she thought.

He left them immediately afterwards.

"I wish he didn't have to leave so suddenly," thought Emma. "I'm happy we parted good friends, however."

The following day, a letter arrived at Randalls to announce[4] the death of Mrs Churchill! It was a sad event[5]—a great shock.

"Poor Mrs Churchill, she really was ill!"

---

1 call on 拜訪
2 let it go 放手
3 change one's mind 改變心意
4 announce [əˈnaʊns] (v.) 宣布
5 event [ɪˈvɛnt] (n.) 事件

Chapter 12

One morning, about ten days after Mrs Churchill's death, Emma was called downstairs to see Mr Weston.

He wanted to speak to her urgently[1]. "Can you come to Randalls this morning? Mrs Weston wants to see you," he said.

"Is she unwell[2]?"

"No, not at all—only a little upset. Can you come?"

"Of course. But what's the matter?"

"Don't ask me. I promised my wife not to tell you."

They set off immediately, and they were soon at Randalls.

"Well, my dear," he said, as they entered the sitting room. "I've brought her." And Emma heard him add, in a whisper, "I've kept my promise[3]. She has no idea[4]."

Mrs Weston looked ill.

"What's the matter?" asked Emma.

"Can't you guess, my dear Emma?" said Mrs Weston in a trembling[5] voice.

"I guess it's something to do with[6] Mr Frank Churchill."

"Yes, it is. He was here this morning. He came to speak to his father—to tell us that he's in love." She stopped. Emma thought first of herself.

---

1 urgently [ˈɝdʒəntlɪ] (adv.) 急迫地
2 unwell [ʌnˈwɛl] (a.) 身體有恙的
3 keep one's promise 信守承諾
4 have no idea 不知道
5 trembling [ˈtrɛmblɪŋ] (a.) 發抖的
6 something to do with 和……有關

"He's engaged[7]," continued Mrs Weston. "Frank Churchill and Miss Fairfax are engaged. In fact they've been engaged for a long time!"

Emma jumped with surprise and exclaimed, "Jane Fairfax! You're not serious!"

"It's true," replied Mrs Weston. "They've been engaged since October—engaged at Weymouth. They kept it a secret from everybody. Nobody knew about it. They tricked[8] us all. We can't forgive his behavior towards you."

Emma thought for a moment, and then she replied, "I'm not in love with him. You must believe me, Mrs Weston. That's the truth."

Mrs Weston kissed her with tears of joy. "Mr Weston will be relieved," she said. "We've been miserable about this. We wanted you to fall in love with each other and we thought that you were in love."

"I've escaped, and we should be grateful[9]," said Emma. "But I can't forgive him, Mrs Weston. He had no right to flirt with me, as he did while he was engaged to somebody else. How did he know that I wasn't falling in love with him?"

"From something that he said, my dear Emma, I think . . ."

"And how could *she* bear such behavior! To watch while he flirted with another woman, in front of her."

---

7 engaged [ɪnˈgedʒd] (a.) 訂了婚的
8 trick [trɪk] (v.) 哄騙
9 grateful [ˈgretfəl] (a.) 感激的

"There were misunderstandings[1] between them, Emma. He said so. He didn't have time to explain much. He was only here for fifteen minutes. He'll write to me soon," continued Mrs Weston. "Let's wait for his letter. It may explain things."

"What did Mr Churchill say?" asked Emma.

"He agreed to the marriage. While Mrs Churchill was alive, there was no hope, no possibility[2]. Frank talked to Mr Churchill last night, and then he left early this morning. He stopped at Highbury to see Jane, and then he came here."

"Well," said Emma, "I wish them happiness."

Jane and Mr Churchill

- Did you guess? Which pages gave you clues[3]?

---

1 misunderstanding [ˌmɪsʌndəˈstændɪŋ] (n.) 誤解
2 possibility [ˌpɑsəˈbɪlətɪ] (n.) 可能性
3 clue [klu] (n.) 線索
4 talent [ˈtælənt] (n.) 天分
5 slightest [ˈslaɪtɪst] (a.) 最微少的

Chapter 13

Later that day, Emma was expecting a visit from her friend, Harriet.

"Poor Harriet!" thought Emma. "She can't marry Frank Churchill now."

"Well, Miss Woodhouse!" cried Harriet, coming quickly into the room. "I've heard the strangest news!"

"What news do you mean?" replied Emma.

"About Jane Fairfax and Mr Frank Churchill. Mr Weston's just told me."

Harriet didn't seem upset by the news. "Had you any idea," cried Harriet, "that he was in love with her? Perhaps, you did. You can see into everybody's heart."

"I'm beginning to doubt I have such talent[4]," said Emma. "I didn't have the slightest[5] idea, till an hour ago. I'm so sorry, Harriet."

"But why are you sorry?" cried Harriet, surprised. "You don't think I like Mr Frank Churchill."

"But you recently told me that you liked him," replied Emma.

"Him! Never."

"But you told me that he was very kind to you, and you had feelings for him. I told you that I wasn't surprised."

"Oh, dear," cried Harriet, "now I remember. But I wasn't thinking of Mr Frank Churchill. No! I was thinking of Mr Knightley. He asked me to dance at the ball when nobody else wanted to dance with me. I'm in love with Mr Knightley."

Emma was shocked. "But do you think Mr Knightley is in love with you?"

"Yes," replied Harriet, "I do."

Emma sat silently, for a few minutes. Why was it so terrible that Harriet was in love with Mr Knightley? Then she understood. "I'm in love with Mr Knightley, too!"

An unhappy Emma listened to Harriet's explanations[1]. After the ball, Harriet noticed that Mr Knightley talked to her much more than before, and he was kinder to her! When they all walked together, he often came and walked by her. He seemed to want to get to know her.

Emma knew that was true. Harriet repeated expressions[2] of praise from him and Emma knew they were true, too. She felt miserable.

Just then, Emma's father came into the room, so they stopped talking.

The rest of the day, and the following night, Emma was upset. She sat still. She walked about. She tried her own room. She tried the garden. She wanted to understand, to completely[3] understand her own heart.

"How long have I been in love with Mr Knightley? When did he replace[4] Frank Churchill?" She thought back. "I *never* loved Frank Churchill! It was *always* Mr Knightley. If Mr Knightley marries Harriet, it will be my fault. I introduced them. Oh, please, don't let him marry. If he never marries, I'll be happy."

Emma knew she couldn't marry Mr Knightley, even if he asked her. She couldn't leave her father alone at Hartfield.

Emma and Mr Knightley

- Did you guess that Emma was in love with Mr Knightley?
- Which pages gave you clues?
- Who do you think Mr Knightley is in love with?

1 explanation [ˌɛkspləˈneʃən] (n.) 解釋
2 expression [ɪkˈsprɛʃən] (n.) 表達；措辭
3 completely [kəmˈplitlɪ] (adv.) 完全地
4 replace [rɪˈples] (v.) 取代

Chapter 14

The next morning, a sadness hung over[1] Hartfield. But in the afternoon, the sun appeared[2], and Emma decided to go outside.

She hurried into the garden. And there, to her surprise, she saw Mr Knightley walking through the garden gate, and walking towards her.

"I must be calm," she told herself.

In half a minute, they were together. Their greeting was awkward[3]. She asked after their family and friends in London. They were all well. When did he leave them? Only that morning. He must have had a wet ride. Yes.

He neither looked nor spoke cheerfully.

"Perhaps he's told his brother about his plans to marry Harriet, and his brother has disapproved[4]," Emma thought.

They walked together. He was silent. He kept looking at her. Perhaps he wanted to speak to her about his feelings for Harriet. She didn't want him to. Yet she couldn't bear this silence. With him it was very unnatural[5]. She thought about it—decided—and, trying to smile, began, "I have some news that will surprise you."

---

1 hang over 籠罩
2 appear [ə`pɪr] (v.) 出現
3 awkward [`ɔkwəd] (a.) 笨拙的
4 disapprove [͵dɪsə`pruv] (v.) 不贊成
5 unnatural [ʌn`nætʃərəl] (a.) 不自然的

🎧 54

"Have you?" he said quietly, "Of what kind?"

"Oh! The best kind in the world—a wedding."

"If you mean Miss Fairfax and Frank Churchill, I've heard that already."

"How?" cried Emma.

"Mr Weston wrote to me this morning, and at the end of the note, he gave me a brief[1] account[2] of what's happened."

"*You* were probably less surprised than any of us, because you had your suspicions. I haven't forgotten that you once tried to warn[3] me about him and I didn't listen to you."

For a moment or two nothing was said, and then she found her arm in his, and held against his heart, and she heard him saying, "Time, my dearest Emma, you'll forget about him in time."

Her arm was held again, "Emma, I'm so sorry. I feel so angry with him. Don't worry! He'll soon be gone. They'll soon be in Yorkshire. I'm sorry for *her*. She could find somebody better."

Emma understood him and she replied, "You're very kind, but you're mistaken. I'm not upset. I'm ashamed of my behavior, but that's all."

"Emma!" he cried. "Is that all?" He stopped. "No, I understand; forgive me. You're right. You'll get over him! I was never sure how much in love with him you were—I only knew you liked him—and I didn't think he was good enough for you."

(55) "Mr Knightley," said Emma, "I've never been in love with Frank Churchill."

He listened in silence. She wanted him to speak, but he didn't.

She went on. "He was the son of Mr Weston, he was continually here. I always found him very pleasant, and," with a sigh[4], "he flattered me. But I've never loved him. And now I understand, he never wanted me to love him. He flirted with me to hide his real feelings for Jane."

She hoped for an answer here, but he was silent, and deep in thought.

At last, he said, "I've never had a high opinion of Frank Churchill, but, for Jane's sake[5], I'll wish him well."

"I'm sure they'll be happy together," said Emma. "I believe they're very much in love."

---

1 brief [brif] (a.) 簡短的
2 account [əˋkaunt] (n.) 解釋；說明
3 warn [wɔrn] (v.) 提醒
4 sigh [saɪ] (n.) 嘆息
5 for one's sake 看在某人的份上

"He's a very lucky man!" said Mr Knightley. "So early in life—at twenty-three—a time when, if a man chooses a wife, he generally chooses badly. Frank Churchill is very lucky. He meets a young woman at the seaside. She falls in love with him. He can't even put her off[1] by flirting with someone else. His aunt is in the way. His aunt dies. His uncle agrees to the marriage. He's behaved badly towards everybody—but everybody forgives him."

"You speak as if you envied[2] him."

"And I do envy him, Emma."

Emma said nothing. She knew, he was thinking about Harriet. She didn't want him to tell her he was in love with Harriet. She must stop him.

Then Mr Knightley surprised her, by saying, "You won't ask me what I envy. You're not at all curious. You're very wise but *I* can't be wise. Emma, I must tell you, though I'll probably regret it later."

Tell

- What is Mr Knightley trying to tell Emma?
- Have you ever tried to tell someone something difficult?

---

1 put sb off 使某人不高興或不喜歡
2 envy [ˈɛnvɪ] (v.) 羨慕

"Oh! Then, don't tell me," she cried. "Take a little time[1] to think about[2] it."

"Thank you," he said, embarrassed, and he didn't say another word.

Emma couldn't bear to upset him. He wanted to talk to her, she should listen. She could help him decide. She could praise Harriet.

They were in front of the house now.

"Are you going inside[3]?" he asked.

"No," replied Emma. "Let's continue our walk."

And, after a few steps, she added, "It was rude of me to stop you, just now, Mr Knightley. If you want to ask my opinion about anything, as a friend, you may. I'll listen, and I'll tell you exactly what I think."

"As a *friend*!" repeated Mr Knightley. "Emma, that's the word I fear[4]. No, I don't want to. Wait. Yes, why should I stop now? I've gone too far already. Emma, I accept your offer, as a *friend*. Tell me, then, will you ever be able to love me?"

He stopped, and looked into her eyes.

"My dearest Emma," he said, "because dearest you will always be, whatever the outcome[5] of this conversation. My dearest, most beloved Emma, tell me at once. Say no if you must."

Emma couldn't speak. She was too happy.

Speak

- When can't you speak? Tick (✓).
  Ask and answer with a friend.
  ☐ When you are happy.
  ☐ When you are sad.
  ☐ When you are angry.
  ☐ When you are embarrassed.

(58) "I can't make speeches[6], Emma," he continued. "If I loved you less, I might be able to talk about it more. But you know me. Dearest Emma, you understand me."

While he spoke, Emma's mind was busy. She saw that Harriet was nothing; that she, Emma, was everything. She couldn't ask him to love Harriet instead, or tell him she didn't love him.

She spoke. What did she say? The right thing, of course. Girls always do. She said enough to show he didn't need to despair[7] and to encourage[8] him to say more himself.

1 take time 抽時間	5 outcome [ˈaʊtˌkʌm] (n.) 結果；後果
2 think about 考慮	6 make a speech 發表演說
3 inside [ˈɪnˈsaɪd] (adv.) 在裡面	7 despair [dɪˈspɛr] (v.) 絕望；喪失信心
4 fear [fɪr] (v.) 擔心	8 encourage [ɪnˈkɝɪdʒ] (v.) 鼓勵

"I heard about Frank Churchill's engagement[1], and I was worried about you. Hearing that you never loved Frank Churchill, gave me hope that, in time, you might love me. I've passed from complete misery[2], to perfect happiness."

Her change was equal. In this one half-hour they both knew that they were loved, and they were no longer jealous. On his side, there was the jealousy[3] of Frank Churchill.

"My love for you, and jealousy of Frank Churchill started at the same moment," he said. "It was my jealousy of Frank Churchill that made me decide to go to London. I didn't want to watch him flirting with you any more," he said. "I went away to try to forget you. But," he continued, "I went to the wrong place. There was too much happiness in my brother's house. Your sister, Isabella, is too like you. I stayed, however, till I got the letter this morning about Jane Fairfax and Frank Churchill. Then, I couldn't stay any longer. I rode home through the rain and I walked to Hartfield straight after lunch, to see you. Then, you told me that you've never loved him."

Happiness returned to Hartfield. And now as they walked back into the house, Mr Knightley knew she was his own dear Emma.

Happiness

- What is happiness for you? Tell a friend.

1 engagement [ɪnˈgedʒmənt] (n.) 訂婚
2 misery [ˈmɪzərɪ] (n.) 痛苦
3 jealousy [ˈdʒɛləsɪ] (n.) 妒忌

Chapter 15

It was time for Emma to break the news[1] to her father!

"Mr Knightley and I are going to get married and *he* is going to come and live at Hartfield," she said.

It was a big shock to her father at first.

"But Father, I'm not leaving Hartfield. I'm staying here," said Emma. "And you'll be much happier having Mr Knightley here."

"Yes. That's very true," her father agreed.

The news was a surprise to everybody. Most people approved of the match. Some thought him lucky, and others thought her lucky.

One evening, Emma visited Randalls with her father. When they arrived, Mrs Weston was in the sitting room with Frank Churchill and Miss Fairfax.

Emma was very happy to see Frank Churchill, but at first, they were both a little embarrassed.

Frank Churchill came over to talk to her. "Thank you, Miss Woodhouse, for your very kind forgiving message in one of Mrs Weston's letters," he said.

"Congratulations on your engagement," said Emma.

---

1 break the news 透露消息

He thanked her again. Then looking at Jane, he said, "Doesn't she look well?" He paused and then asked, "But didn't you ever have any suspicion about Jane and I?"

"No, never," replied Emma.

"I'm surprised. I nearly told you everything once. I wish I had."

"It doesn't matter now," said Emma. "But tell me. Did you send the piano to Jane?"

"Yes, I did," he said with a smile. "I bought it that day in London."

"Nobody guessed it was from you. We even thought it was from Mr Knightley!"

"Ah!" he said, "I hope Mr Knightley is well." He paused.

She blushed and laughed.

"Congratulations. I was very happy to hear the news," said Frank Churchill.

Then his thoughts turned to Jane again, and he said, "Did you ever see such a beautiful face!"

"I've always thought she was beautiful," replied Emma, "but I remember you thought she was too pale. Have you forgotten?"

He laughed, and Emma said, "I think you enjoyed tricking us all."

"Oh, no! I was miserable!" he said.

62   Emma was happy to see Frank Churchill, but she left Randalls that evening, more in love with Mr Knightley than ever.

In October, that year, Emma and Mr Knightley got married. The wishes and hopes, of the small group of friends at the wedding, were all answered in the perfect happiness of the marriage.

Ⓐ Personal Response

1 Did you like the story? Why / why not?

2 Who was your favorite character? Give reasons.

3 Who did you want Emma to marry? Give reasons.

4 In your opinion, what is a good match? Tick (✓).
Somebody with _____

- ☐ ⓐ youth and beauty.
- ☐ ⓑ wit and intelligence.
- ☐ ⓒ kindness and generosity.

5 Read these quotes from Jane Austen. What do they tell us about Jane Austen and the time she lived in? Discuss in pairs.

- ⓐ "Single women were generally poor. Which is one very strong argument in favor of marriage."
- ⓑ "Let other pens write about guilt and misery."
- ⓒ "Every man is surrounded by a neighborhood of voluntary spies."

6 Read this quote by another famous author, Charlotte Brontë (1816–55). Do you agree? Discuss in pairs.

"I wouldn't like to live with Jane Austen's ladies and gentlemen, in their elegant but confined houses."

❸ Comprehension

7 Tick (✓) true (T) or false (F).

T **F** (a) Emma didn't want Miss Taylor to marry Mr Weston.
T **F** (b) Mr Dixon saved Jane Fairfax from drowning.
T **F** (c) Mr Knightley sent the piano to Jane Fairfax.
T **F** (d) Mr Knightley was jealous of Frank Churchill.
T **F** (e) Emma wasn't good friends with Jane Fairfax.
T **F** (f) Mr and Mrs Weston didn't want Frank Churchill to marry Emma.

8 Put the events from the story into the correct order.

☐ (a) Frank Churchill tells the Westons that he is engaged to Jane Fairfax.
☐ (b) Frank Churchill comes to Highbury and he meets Emma.
☐ (c) Jane Fairfax comes to stay with her aunt in Highbury.
1 (d) Emma's governess, Miss Taylor, marries Mr Weston.
☐ (e) Frank Churchill cancels his visit to Highbury.
☐ (f) Mrs Weston tells Emma about Frank Churchill's engagement.
☐ (g) Mr Weston's son, Frank Churchill, plans a visit to Highbury.
☐ (h) Emma thinks that Frank Churchill is in love with her.
☐ (i) Emma tells Mrs Weston that she is not in love with Frank Churchill.
☐ (j) Emma marries Mr Knightley.

9 Agree (✓) or disagree (×) with the statements.
Explain your choice to a friend.

☐ a Mr Knightley is very kind.

☐ b Emma is a good match-maker.

☐ c Frank Churchill shouldn't flirt with Emma.

☐ d Jane Fairfax should tell Emma that she is engaged to Frank Churchill.

☐ e Mr Knightley will be a good husband for Emma.

☐ f It is easy to match-make people.

10 Match the female characters to the men they are in love with.

Mr Knightley

Mr Weston

Frank Churchill

Emma

Harriet

Jane Fairfax

Miss Taylor

C Characters

11 Circle the words that describe Mr Knightley.

- ☐ kind
- ☐ mysterious
- ☐ secretive
- ☐ good-looking
- ☐ selfish
- ☐ vain
- ☐ ugly
- ☐ short
- ☐ thirty-seven
- ☐ twenty-six
- ☐ modest
- ☐ generous

12 Now complete the short description of Mr Knightley using the words from Exercise **11**.

Mr Knightley is (a) _____ years old. He has got dark hair and he is (b) _____. He likes to help people. He is very (c) _____ and (d) _____. He does a lot of good deeds, but he doesn't like to talk about them. He is very (e) _____.

13 Complete the paragraph about the characters with the words below.

son
father
brother
aunt
neighbor
uncle
governess
son
wife
sister

Mr Knightley lives in a large house near Emma and her [a] _____ , Mr Woodhouse. He is their [b] _____.

His [c] _____ is married to Emma's [d] _____, Isabella, and they have a [e] _____, Henry. Emma's [f] _____, Miss Taylor, has just got married to Mr Weston. Mr Weston's first [g] _____ died, and his [h] _____ Frank lives with his [i] _____, Mrs Churchill and his [j] _____, Mr Churchill.

14 Write the name of the correct character next to the sentences.

[a] He never flatters Emma. _____

[b] He hates change and marriage brings change. _____

[c] She has decided, she will never marry. _____

[d] He flirts with Emma in front of everybody. _____

[e] She is secretly engaged to Frank Churchill. _____

[f] She falls in love with Mr Knightley when he dances with her. _____

15 Write the name of the correct character next to Emma's thoughts.

a) I couldn't be friends with anyone so shy _____
and secretive.

b) We get on so well and we think so alike. _____

c) He's secretly in love with Jane Fairfax. _____

d) He doesn't need to marry. He's happy as _____
a single man.

16 Write a sentence to describe each of these characters. Compare with a friend.

Emma

Jane Fairfax

Mr Knightley

Frank Churchill

17 Do you like the characters in Exercise **16**? Why / why not? Discuss with a friend.

D Plot and Theme

18 There are lots of misunderstandings in the story and the reader is constantly tested about what is happening and how the characters feel. Choose the correct words.

a. Frank Churchill was in love / flirted with Emma.

b. Frank Churchill flattered / married Emma.

c. Frank Churchill was / was not in love with Jane Fairfax.

d. Harriet was engaged to / in love with Mr Knightley.

e. Mr Knightley always criticized / flattered Emma.

f. Emma fell in love / flirted with Mr Knightley.

g. Mr Knightley asked Emma to marry / flatter him.

h. Emma got married to / forgot Mr Knightley in the end.

19 Emma thinks some people are in love. Is she right? Read the sentences and mark them right (✓) or wrong (✗). Correct the "wrong" sentences.

☐ a. Harriet is in love with Frank Churchill.

☐ b. Mr Dixon is in love with Jane Fairfax.

☐ c. Frank Churchill loves Jane Fairfax.

☐ d. Frank Churchill is in love with Emma.

☐ e. Mr Weston is a good husband for Miss Taylor.

☐ f. Mr Knightley doesn't love Jane Fairfax.

☐ g. Mr Knightley loves Harriet.

20 Now read the quote. Is it true? Write Yes or No.

"You (Emma) can see into everybody's heart." _____

21 Read the quote and discuss the questions in small groups of four.

"True love and a good marriage can only happen if you choose someone of an equal position in society, equal education and equal good looks."

Frank Churchill   Jane Fairfax

1 Do you think this is true of Jane Fairfax (see page 24) and Frank Churchill (see page 19)?

Emma   Mr Knightley

3 What you think about true love?

2 And of Emma (see page 15) and Mr Knightley (see page 16)?

22 Find **10** mistakes in the story summary and underline them.

The story takes place in the big city of Highbury. The main character is Emma. Emma believes that she is very good at match-making. She enjoys imagining that people are in love with each other, but she is usually wrong. She is even wrong about herself.

One day, Frank Churchill, a very ugly young man comes to stay with Emma's sister, Mrs Weston. Frank is the nephew of Mr Weston, her husband. Emma imagines that everyone must want her to marry Frank Churchill. She herself thinks they are a good match. Sadly, she isn't in love with him. However, she believes that he is in love with her. They flirt together and everyone thinks that they are in love.

Later, they find out that Frank Churchill has tricked them all. He is secretly married to Jane Fairfax. He flirted with Emma to hide the fact that he is in love with Jane. When he announces his marriage to his father and Mrs Weston, they are very happy. They think the news will hurt Emma. Mr Knightley also thinks that Emma will be happy. By this time, Emma knows that she is in love with Mr Elton. Fortunately, he is in love with Emma. And so the story ends very sadly with the marriage of Emma and Mr Knightley.

🎧 63 **23** Now listen and check your answers.

🄴 Language

24 Match the adjectives from the novel with their synonyms.

1. very surprised
2. helpful and good
3. very unhappy
4. wanting something somebody else has
5. thinking you are good-looking

☐ (a) miserable

☐ (b) shocked

☐ (c) jealous

☐ (d) vain

☐ (e) kind

25 Now complete the sentences with the adjectives from Exercise **24**.

(a) Everybody was _____ when they learnt that Frank Churchill was engaged to Jane Fairfax.

(b) Emma thought Frank Churchill was _____ because he went to London to have his hair cut.

(c) Mr Knightley was _____ of Frank Churchill because he thought Emma was in love with him.

(d) Mr Knightley was very _____. He sent his carriage to take Miss Bates and Miss Fairfax to the dinner party at the Coles's house.

(e) Emma was _____ when she thought Mr Knightley was in love with Harriet.

26 Write sentences comparing the characters using the adjectives and example below.

> handsome
> beautiful
> kind
> good

Mr Knightley is more handsome than the other men standing with him at the ball.

27 Match the everyday expressions from the novel with their meanings.

1. I caused this a problem.
2. Everybody looked after her.
3. I really want to meet him.
4. I did it for your good.
5. You talk too much.
6. I am very good friends with her.

- [ ] a. I'm dying to meet him.
- [ ] b. You're such a chatterbox.
- [ ] c. I get on so well with her.
- [ ] d. I did it for your sake.
- [ ] e. Everybody made a fuss of her.
- [ ] f. It's my fault.

28 Complete the sentences with the past passive of the verbs below.

eg Emma had servants to do everything for her.

iron
cook
drive
look after
teach

a Her carriage _____ for her.

b Her meals _____ for her.

c Her horses _____ for her.

d Her clothes _____ for her.

e She didn't go to school.
She _____ by a governess.

29 Write another sentence about Emma using the past passive.

....

....

....

....

TEST

 1 Choose the correct answer 1, 2, 3 or 4.

_____ a Emma has got _____.

1 two sisters

2 a brother

3 a sister

4 a brother and a sister

_____ b Jane Fairfax is staying in Highbury with Miss Bates, her _____.

1 mother

2 aunt

3 sister

4 friend

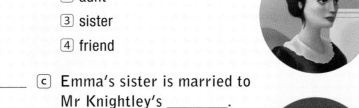

_____ c Emma's sister is married to Mr Knightley's _____.

1 brother

2 father

3 friend

4 uncle

_____ d Emma loves _____.

1 match-making

2 playing the piano

3 singing

4 being alone

_____ e Emma's father doesn't like _____.

1 balls
2 picnics
3 smoking
4 change

_____ f Whose first wife dies?

1 Mr Knightley's.
2 Frank Churchill's.
3 Mr Weston's.
4 Mr Dixon's.

_____ g Mr Knightley is very _____.

1 selfish
2 thoughtful and kind
3 vain
4 funny

2 Answer the following questions.

- (a) In which century was *Emma* written?
- (b) Who gives the piano to Jane Fairfax?
- (c) Who does Mrs Weston think gives the piano to Jane Fairfax?
- (d) Who does Emma think gives the piano to Jane Fairfax?
- (e) Who saves Jane Fairfax when she nearly falls out of the boat?
- (f) Whose visit to Highbury is everybody excited about?
- (g) Why does Frank Churchill cancel his visit to Highbury?
- (h) What is Mrs Churchill's relationship to Frank Churchill?
- (i) What two letters are perfection in Mr Weston's riddle?
- (j) When does Harriet fall in love with Mr Knightley?
- (k) Who do Mr and Mrs Weston want Frank Churchill to marry?
- (l) Why doesn't Emma's father like weddings?
- (m) When does Emma realize that she's in love with Mr Knightley?
- (n) Does the story have a happy ending?

Heroes and heroines

1 Complete the quiz. Compare your answers with a friend.

Could you be a Jane Austen heroine?

_____ [a] How well can you play the piano?
   1 Very well.   2 Quite well.   3 Not at all.

_____ [b] How well can you paint?
   1 Very well.   2 Quite well.   3 Not at all.

_____ [c] How well can you sew?
   1 Very well.   2 Quite well.   3 Not at all.

_____ [d] Do you like spending time with friends?
   1 Yes.   2 No.   3 Not at all.

_____ [e] Would you like to organize a dinner party or a ball?
   1 Yes.   2 No.   3 Definitely not.

2 Could you be a Jane Austen hero?
In pairs, write your own quiz for boys.

3 Think of and describe a modern 21st-century hero /
heroine. Include details of character, clothes, interests,
daily life and routine. Make a poster and add pictures.
Use the Internet to help you.

作者簡介 珍‧奧斯汀出生於 1775 年 12 月，有七名兄弟姊妹，家中排行倒數第二。奧斯汀一家住在漢普夏的史蒂文頓，父親是教區牧師，這是一個快樂、教養良好、溫馨的家庭。

珍‧奧斯汀十二歲就開始為家人寫故事，她在青少年時期就立志當作家。珍‧奧斯汀的所有小說都對婚姻有所著墨，但她本身一生小姑獨處。她和一位學法律的年輕人湯姆‧列夫羅伊有過一段情，但男方之後另娶同學的姊妹。老友哈里斯‧彼格威瑟曾向她求婚，但她並不愛他，也沒有接受求婚。她在寫給姪女芬妮的信中說道：「你能做的最糟糕的事情，就是嫁給自己不愛的人。」這種看法在當時並不是常態，對一八〇〇年代的大部分女性來說，愛情沒有財富或良好的社會地位來得重要。

珍‧奧斯汀在很短的時間內就寫成了六部出色的小說。《理性與感性》寫於 1811 年，《傲慢與偏見》寫於 1813 年，《曼斯菲爾德莊園》寫於 1814 年，《艾瑪》寫於 1814–15 年，《諾桑覺寺》和《勸導》則是在她過世後的 1817 年才出版。這些小說都是匿名出版，但她還在世時，人們就已經知道她是作者。攝政王是她的小說迷，還希望她把《艾瑪》一書獻給他。

1816 年，珍‧奧斯汀罹病。 1817 年 7 月，她於溫徹斯特辭世，長眠於溫徹斯特大教堂。

本書簡介 珍‧奧斯汀於 1814 年 1 月開始撰寫《艾瑪》，1815 年 3 月完成。之後在 1815 年 12 月由約翰‧穆瑞出版，穆瑞也出版過詩人拜倫勳爵的作品。這部小說分成三冊出版。

珍‧奧斯汀有一個有名的建言，她跟姪女建議說：三、四個鄉間村落的家庭，是小說的最佳題材。而她寫的內容也正是如此。《艾瑪》的背景設定在英國南方的小村落海布里，描述村落中一小群人的關係：艾瑪、奈特利先生、法蘭克‧邱吉爾、珍‧費法，以及他們的親朋好友。

在當時，年輕女子的志向就是盡可能嫁一個好人家，故事的主人翁艾瑪卻決心不結婚。這並不尋常，因為女人的職責就是嫁人。不過艾瑪家財萬貫，不愁要嫁人。

《艾瑪》的道德主題是社會秩序的存在，小說中違反社會規範的角色，最後落得的下場不是生病，就是不幸。人要誠實面對人際關係，不然無有幸福可言。人要幸福，就要融入自己生活的社群之中，並且親切有禮地對待社群中的每一個人。我們從小說中學到，選擇的對象在社會地位、教育程度和外表上都要門戶相當，才有真愛和良緣可言。

艾瑪以為有幾個角色彼此鍾愛，但她卻總是猜錯。她憑藉的是自己的想像力，以為愛情就像當時的羅曼史小說所描繪的那樣，而這正是珍‧奧斯汀所不喜歡的。

第一章

P. 15

艾瑪‧伍德豪斯快樂、美麗、聰明又富有。二十一歲時,她的生活無憂無慮。她是慈愛的父親伍德豪斯先生的么女。姐姐伊莎貝拉已嫁作人婦,住在倫敦。父親是鰥夫,艾瑪便成了家裡的女主人。

艾瑪五歲時,媽媽就過世,由和藹可親的家庭教師泰勒小姐,將艾瑪和伊莎貝拉拉拔長大。泰勒小姐很疼愛這一對女兒,尤其是艾瑪。她們一起生活,相處起來像朋友,艾瑪可以隨心所欲地做她想做的事。

泰勒小姐結婚時,不幸之感才終於降臨。泰勒小姐與韋斯頓先生的婚姻很幸福,艾瑪也很喜歡泰勒小姐的丈夫。不過她現在感到淒涼,她在家裡已經沒有朋友了,她很想念泰勒小姐。

艾瑪的父親不喜歡改變,而婚姻帶來了改變。泰勒小姐婚禮結束的那天晚上,艾瑪陪父親坐著,盡量談笑自如。

P. 16

然而,茶端來的時候,伍德豪斯先生說:「可憐的泰勒小姐!真希望她在這裡。韋斯頓先生想娶她,真是遺憾!」

艾瑪說:「我不贊成你說的。泰勒小姐總不能永遠跟我們住在一起,她現在有她自己的房子了。」

「她自己的房子!她何必要有自己的房子?這間房子比他們的房子大上三倍。」

「我們可以常常去找他們,他們也會來看我們。」艾瑪保證道。

艾瑪想解父親的愁,便決定來玩盤雙陸棋。就在她準備棋桌時,一位訪客走了進來。那是奈特利先生,他很英俊,年約三十七歲。他是艾瑪家的好友,也是伊莎貝拉的丈夫的哥哥。他住在離哈費一英哩外的地方,經常來訪。伍德豪斯先生很高興見到他。

P. 17

「希望婚禮進行得順利。」奈特利先生說:「誰哭得最慘啊?」

「啊!是可憐的泰勒小姐!」伍德豪斯先生說。

「可憐的不是泰勒小姐,而是伍德豪斯先生和伍德豪斯小姐。只照顧一個丈夫,想必比照顧你們兩個人來得好些。」奈特利先生說。

「尤其那兩個人當中還有一個特別難搞的,你想說的是這個吧。」艾瑪打趣地說。

「這是實話，我有時候很不好相處吧。」伍德豪斯先生說。

「父親，我不是在說你，我是在說我自己。奈特利先生就愛挑我毛病。」

奈特利先生是少數能看到艾瑪·伍德豪斯的缺點的人，也只有他會直言不諱。

「艾瑪知道我是不會巴結她的。」奈特利先生說。

「艾瑪會很想念泰勒小姐。」她的父親說道。

「艾瑪當然會想念她了，但泰勒小姐所有的朋友一定都為她幸福地出嫁感到高興。」奈特利先生說。

P.18

「你忘了，是我本人幫他們牽線的。」艾瑪說。

奈特利先生對她搖搖頭。

「請別再作媒了，艾瑪。」她的父親說。

「我答應我不幫自己作媒，但我要幫別人湊合。這很有趣。既然我已經成功過了，就不會罷手。」

奈特利先生說：「我不知道你說『成功』是什麼意思。人可以為自己找到丈夫或妻子。」

「請別再作媒了。」伍德豪斯先生說。

「再作一次媒就好，我一定要幫艾爾頓先生找個妻子。」

「如果你真想對艾爾頓先生好，就去找他來吃晚餐。」

「對，艾瑪，邀請他來晚餐，不過就讓他去挑自己妻子吧。都二十六歲的男人，可以自己去找老婆了。」奈特利先生笑著說。

作媒

- 你覺得作媒是好事還是壞事？
- 你曾經試著幫朋友作媒嗎？

第二章

P.19

韋斯頓的第一任妻子，是來自約克夏一個富裕的邱吉爾家族，但婚後三年便過世，留下一個兒子法蘭克。邱吉爾夫婦是法蘭克的舅媽和舅父，他們膝下無子，於是提議要照顧法蘭克。他們都住在蘇格蘭的安斯康柏。

往後的二十年，韋斯頓先生的日子過得很順心。他買下一棟中意的大房子，位在英格蘭南方海布里村一帶，宅邸叫做藍道。他每年和兒子見面一次，非常以兒子為榮。海布里的人也都為法蘭克·邱吉爾感到驕傲，人人都渴望見到他。大家常說他要來看父親，但都虛晃一招。

這下子，艾瑪雖無意結婚，卻常想著自己應該要嫁給法蘭克·邱吉爾，彷彿他是屬於她的。她心想，所有的親朋好友一定都希望他們能夠結婚，她也確定韋斯頓夫婦希望兩人能夠結成一對。她很想能和他見面，打算和他互相鍾情。

艾瑪再次來訪藍道時，聽見了令人興奮的消息。

「法蘭克要來這裡住。」韋斯頓先生帶

她到客廳的時候說:「我今天早上收到他的來信。」

P. 20

艾瑪說:「這真是好消息!韋斯頓太太一定也很高興。」

「是呀,但她認為他不會來。」

艾瑪去和韋斯頓太太談論著這件事。她說:「法蘭克要來訪,得他的舅媽同意才行。他對父親的愛,讓邱吉爾太太很吃醋。」

法蘭克・邱吉爾先生沒有來訪,只送來了一封道歉信。他很遺憾不能來訪,邱吉爾太太需要他留在家裡。韋斯頓夫婦很失望。艾瑪向奈特利先生訴說他們的失望。

「我敢說,他要是真的想來,就會來。」奈特利先生說。

「我不知道你為什麼要這樣說,他是真的想來,但他的舅父和舅媽不讓他來。」

「如果法蘭克・邱吉爾真的想看自己的父親,就可以安排。他已經這麼大了。他幾歲?都二十三或二十四歲了吧。」

「你說得容易。」

「他有錢,又有閒,我們都知道他多的是金錢和時間,老是聽說他去海邊的度假勝地或是哪裡度假了。不久前,他還去了威茅斯,這證明他可以離開邱吉爾家。」

「有時候是可以沒錯。」

「艾瑪,有件事情是男人一定能做的,那就是他的天職。拜訪父親,是法蘭克・邱吉爾的天職,他應該對邱吉爾夫人說,我一定要去看我父親。如果我不去看他,他會很難過。」

P. 21

法蘭克・邱吉爾

■法蘭克是什麼人?勾選正確的框框。

☐ 韋斯頓先生第一次婚姻所生的兒子。
☐ 泰勒小姐的兒子。
☐ 邱吉爾夫婦的姪兒。
☐ 邱吉爾家的兒子。

「法蘭克・邱吉爾先生不能那樣對舅父和舅媽說話。」

「那他就是個軟弱的年輕人。」奈特利先生說。

艾瑪大聲說:「我確定他才不是軟弱的年輕人。你好像就是要把他想得很壞。」

奈特利先生回答:「我才沒有!我是很想說他的好話,只是還沒聽過他有什麼好的,除了他長得又高又帥,還有,他很有禮貌。」

「那麼他在海布里就會很受歡迎了,我們這裡又高又帥的年輕人並不多見。如果他來訪,唐維爾和海布里的人們就會只有一個話題——法蘭克・邱吉爾先生。」

P. 22

「我要是覺得他聰明,就會樂意跟他交朋友。不過如果他虛有其表,只會嘰哩呱啦,本人就不奉陪了。」

「我想他可以跟每一個人都處得來,大家都會喜歡他。他可以和你耕農作,和我聊繪畫或音樂,可以和每一個人都有話聊。這是我對他的看法。」艾瑪說。

「我的看法是,如果真是這樣,那他就太糟糕了。」奈特利先生說。

「我不說他的事了。」艾瑪大聲說：「我們兩人都有成見，你覺得他不好，我覺得他很好。」

「成見？我才沒有成見，我根本就沒去想這個人。」奈特利先生說。

艾瑪不解奈特利先生幹嘛發火，而且奈特利先生不像是會去討厭還沒見過面的人。

第三章

P. 23

隔天，艾瑪來到海布里村，便決定去拜訪貝茨太太和小姐。她們喜歡訪客來訪，奈特利先生常告訴艾瑪，應該要更常去拜訪她們。

因此那天上午，艾瑪陪她們坐了一個鐘頭。跟平常一樣，她們聊天的內容很快就轉向她們的姪女珍·費法。

「我們今天早上收到了珍的來信。」貝茨小姐說。

「希望她安好。」艾瑪禮貌地說道。

「她很好。」貝茨小姐一邊找信，一邊答道。「哦，在這裡。不過我要先道個歉，信很短，只有兩頁。」

艾瑪想著能否逃離。

「珍上次來，是兩年前的事了，對吧。」貝茨小姐說。

「珍要過來住嗎？」

「是呀，下個星期。」

「那真是好消息。」艾瑪說。

「沒錯。她會來住三個月。坎貝爾上校和夫人要去愛爾蘭，和女兒迪克森太太和先生一起住。迪克森先生是很好的

年輕人，他在威茅斯救了珍一命。當時他們在船上，她差點被拋到海裡。我想到這件事就發抖！我們聽說了這件事以後，我就很喜歡迪克森先生。珍下星期五或六都會來到這裡。我好興奮！我們現在就來看她的信吧，由她自己來講她自己的事，一定比我講得精彩多了。」

P. 24

「我想我得走了。」艾瑪匆忙說道，因為她不想重覆聽那封信的內容。「我父親在家裡等我，我現在得告辭了。」

珍·費法的雙親在她小時候就過世，她便去和祖母、姨媽同住。後來，她父親的一個朋友改變了她的命運，這位朋友是坎貝爾上校。

九歲時，珍去和坎貝爾家住。他們有一個女兒坎貝爾小姐，她和珍同年齡，兩人成了好朋友。珍很幸運，她在那裡受到了良好的教育。

後來，坎貝爾小姐和合意的年輕小伙子迪克森先生相戀，兩人爾後成親。

珍今年二十一歲，她想工作，也有教小孩的資格。她要來海布里與姨媽和祖母享受最後幾個月的自由。

海布里的人沒能歡喜地迎接法蘭克·邱吉爾先生，反倒要包容珍·費法了。

要對不喜歡的人以禮相待三個月，艾瑪感到難過。她為什麼不喜歡珍·費法？這難以回答。奈特利先生說，那是因為艾瑪希望自己也能成為像珍那樣的人。

P. 26

她當時不認同他的話，但她知道自己被說中了。此外還有其他的原因，珍冷

冷淡淡的，顧忌心重，而且大家都對她大驚小怪。大家都認為她們應該要成為朋友，因為兩人的年紀相當。

珍·費法才剛抵達，艾瑪就去拜訪。珍·費法高䠒優雅，有一頭深色的頭髮，皮膚蒼白，一雙深邃的灰色眼睛，有著深色的睫毛和眉毛。她比艾瑪記憶中的樣子來得更漂亮。

第一次拜訪時，艾瑪就決定她不能再討厭珍了。她覺得可惜，在海布里沒有合適的年輕人可以和珍結婚，她找不到對象幫珍作媒。

然而，這樣的好感沒有持續太久。珍與祖母和姨媽在哈費過夜，那天晚上，珍沒有對任何事情表達自己內心真正的想法，特別是講到威茅斯和迪克森家的話題時，更是多所保留。

艾瑪覺得珍有所隱瞞。也許迪克森先生真正喜歡的人是珍，搞不好他選擇娶坎貝爾小姐，只是因為覬覦女方的家產。

P. 27

珍對於其他的話題也遮遮掩掩的。她和法蘭克·邱吉爾先生同時都待在威茅斯，艾瑪知道他們稍有認識，可是從珍那裡根本打聽不出來法蘭克是什麼樣的人。

「他長得帥嗎？」

她相信，大家都會覺得他很帥。

「他討人喜歡嗎？」

她相信，大家都會覺得他很有禮貌。

「他聰明嗎？」

她跟邱吉爾先生還沒那麼熟，無法評論。

艾瑪無法寬恕她。

隱瞞

▪ 你能夠和有所隱瞞的人做朋友嗎？
▪ 隱瞞，是好還是壞？進行小組討論。

第四章

P. 28

隔天早上，艾瑪決定要拜訪韋斯頓家。

她抵達時，韋斯頓先生說：「好消息！法蘭克明天要來，我今天早上收到信，他晚餐前會到達藍道。」

艾瑪笑了笑，向韋斯頓先生道賀。

「我明天晚上會帶他到哈費。」他說。

「哦，好啊，請帶過來。」艾瑪說。

「艾瑪，明天四點左右，要想到我。」韋斯頓太太說道，法蘭克的來訪讓她很緊張。

「好的。」艾瑪說道，然後辭行回家。

到了令人關注的這一天早上，十點、十一點、十二點時，艾瑪都惦記著四點時要想到韋斯頓太太。

十二點時，她打開客廳的門，很驚訝地看見兩位紳士正陪父親坐著，那是韋斯頓先生和他的兒子。

「法蘭克提早一天來。」韋斯頓先生解釋說。

法蘭克·邱吉爾真的來了。他是一位年輕大的大帥哥，看起來很親切，而且為人風趣。艾瑪頓時對他產生好感。

P. 29

法蘭克·邱吉爾喜歡藍道，喜歡這個地點，喜歡那條通往海布里的步道、海布里，還特別讚賞哈費。

他好像很熱切地想認識艾瑪，問了她很多事情：這一帶地區大嗎？她會騎馬嗎？有好的步道嗎？舞會呢？人們會辦舞會嗎？

艾瑪回答了這些所有的問題，接著邱吉爾先生開始談起韋斯頓太太。

他說：「她給我父親帶來幸福，我感激不盡。」

法蘭克·邱吉爾知道如何討人歡心，他一定是想討好艾瑪。

最後他說：「我很驚訝韋斯頓太太那麼年輕漂亮，我沒有想到會是個年輕的美女。」

「別讓她知道你稱她是年輕的美女。」艾瑪笑著說。

「當然不會囉，我和韋斯頓太太談話時，知道應該要讚美誰。」他回答。

P. 31

「那他也知道大家期待我和他湊成一對嗎？」艾瑪心想。她看到韋斯頓先生面露喜悅地看著他們，知道他在聽著他們交談。

如何取悅人

- 你知道如何使人開心嗎？
- 想想看，你做過什麼事來取悅別人。和夥伴分享。

不久，韋斯頓先生起身準備離開，他得辭行去海布里。他的兒子也起身，跟父親說道：「既然你要去海布里，那我就跟著去拜訪一個熟識。我認識你的一位鄰居，一個住在海布里的女士，姓巴恩斯或貝茨。你認識姓貝茨或巴恩斯的人嗎？」

章斯頓先生喊道：「我們當然認識。貝茨太太，我們路過她家，我還看到貝茨小姐就站在窗邊。對了，你認識費法小姐，我記得你是在威茅斯認識她的。你當然要去看看她了。」

P. 32

「我今天早上不一定要去拜訪她，我改天再去。但我們在威茅斯認識，所以……」這位年輕的男子說。

「哦，你就今天去吧，別拖延了。」他的父親說道。

「費法小姐跟我說，她認識你。」艾瑪說：「她是個文雅的年輕姑娘。」。

法蘭克贊同，但只是輕輕地說了聲「是的」，這讓她覺得他言不由衷。

這兩位先生隨即告辭。艾瑪對他們友誼的第一步感到很滿意。

費法小姐
- 費法小姐的名字叫什麼？艾瑪對她的看法如何？請往前翻到第 26–27 頁找答案。

第五章

P. 33

隔天早上，法蘭克·邱吉爾先生再度來訪。這一次，他和章斯頓太太一道過來。艾瑪沒料到他們會來，又驚又喜。她期待能夠再見到法蘭克，尤其想見他

和章斯頓太太在一起。看到他們兩個人一起來，她很開心。法蘭克很重視章斯頓太太對他的關愛和情誼。

他們一起散步到海布里。途中，他們在皇冠客棧逗留。艾瑪跟法蘭克·邱吉爾說起那家由來已久的舞廳，他馬上興致勃勃，透過窗戶往舞廳裡面瞧。

他說：「這裡應該要兩個星期辦一次舞會。伍德豪斯小姐，你怎麼都不在這裡辦舞會呢？我們一定要來辦場舞會。」

他們繼續走，現在快來到了貝茨家的對面。

「你拜訪了貝茨家嗎？」艾瑪問。

他回答：「哦，是的。這次的拜訪很圓滿，三位女士我都拜會了。」

「你覺得費法小姐看上去怎麼樣？」艾瑪問。

「她看起來好像生病了，病得很重。不過，費法小姐本來就很蒼白，所以看起來都好像是生病的樣子。」

P. 34

艾瑪不認同他的話，她說：「她看起來不像是有病容，她白皙的皮膚很漂亮。」

「我是聽很多人這樣說，但我比較喜歡健康的膚色。」他說。

「你在威茅斯時，經常和珍·費法見面嗎？」艾瑪問。

「費法女士沒有回答過這個問題嗎？」

「沒有。但話說回來，她的口風很緊，不會透露別人的事情。」艾瑪說。

「好吧，我就照實說了，我在威茅斯時經常和她見面。」他繼續說道：「現在請跟我說，你聽過費法小姐彈鋼琴嗎？」

「我聽過呀！」艾瑪重複了一聲。「我

每年都聽她彈琴，她琴藝很好。」

「你是這樣想的嗎？」他繼續說道：「我覺得她彈得很好。我記得迪克森先生一直喜歡她彈鋼琴。」

「這讓坎貝爾小姐作何感想？她會吃味嗎？」

「這我就不知道了。他們三個人的感情好像很和諧。」他開始說道，停頓了一會兒後，又補上一句：「但我無法說什麼，你和她比較熟。」

「我們是認識很久了，但一直都不是密友。我無法和那麼有所顧忌和隱瞞的人交朋友。」

「我也不喜歡遮遮掩掩的人，無法喜歡那麼有所顧忌和隱瞞的人。」法蘭克·邱吉爾說。

P. 36

他們相處融洽，想法相近，艾瑪不敢相信她和法蘭克·邱吉爾才見過第二次面而已。

但很可惜的，艾瑪對法蘭克·邱吉爾的好感，隔天就被破壞了，因為她聽到韋斯頓太太說：「他去倫敦剪頭髮了。」

艾瑪覺得這種作風太浮華了，不過除了這一點之外，艾瑪覺得他這個人還是不錯。她為他感到很開心，能愛上她自己，或是說差不多要愛上了。當然，她並不愛他——她才不想嫁人呢。

韋斯頓先生跟艾瑪透露說，法蘭克很喜歡她，覺得她長得很漂亮，這讓艾瑪對他更有好感了。她決定不要對他太挑三撿四。

然而，有個人就不以為然了——奈特利先生。他聽說了理髮的事，艾瑪聽到他說：「哼！早就料到了他是個蠢傢伙。」

第六章

P. 37

法蘭克·邱吉爾剪了頭髮從倫敦回來。他揶揄了自己，但似乎一點也不會難為情。

星期二，柯爾夫婦要舉辦晚宴。

「哦，太好了！機會又來了，可以猜猜法蘭克·邱吉爾對我的感覺。如果他很迷戀我，那我就要對他冷淡一點。」艾瑪心想。

星期二晚上，艾瑪的座車尾隨著另一輛馬車來到柯爾夫婦家。她發現那是奈

特利先生的馬車,這讓她很開心。艾瑪覺得,奈特利先生太少搭馬車了。他等著扶她走下馬車。

「你出門都該是這樣子,像個紳士。」艾瑪說。

他向她道謝說:「我們竟同時到達,真幸運!這下子你知道了吧,我也可以像個紳士。」

「哦,可不是嗎,這一刻我很高興陪你走進同一個房間。」她笑著說道。

「傻女孩!」他回答。

P. 39

紳士

- 你認為奈特利先生是紳士嗎?
  為什麼?跟夥伴分享。

晚餐時,艾瑪坐在法蘭克·邱吉爾旁邊。她整個心思都在他身上,直到她聽到柯爾太太聊起珍的一個有趣事情。

柯爾太太說:「我今天下午去找貝茨小姐時,看到了一架鋼琴,是今天早上送到的。珍不知道是誰送來的,他們覺得包準是坎貝爾上校。不過,珍最近才收到坎貝爾家寄來的信,信上並沒有提到鋼琴的事。」

大家都同意一定是坎貝爾上校送來的。

艾瑪轉身面向法蘭克·邱吉爾。

「你在笑什麼?」她問。

「我沒有呀,是你先笑的。你在笑什麼?」

「我嗎?我覺得很奇怪呀,他以前沒送過鋼琴給她。」艾瑪說。

「大概是因為費法小姐以前不會在這裡待那麼久。」法蘭克·邱吉爾回答。

P. 40

「你想的和我想的一樣,我知道你在想什麼!」艾瑪說。

「有可能喔。那跟我說你現在在想什麼。」法蘭克·邱吉爾說。

「我在想,鋼琴是迪克森先生送來的。」艾瑪說。

「迪克森先生——對,有可能是迪克森夫婦送來的禮物。我那天跟你說過,他很欣賞她的演奏。」

「是的,這證實了我的想法。我猜迪克森先生在向坎貝爾小姐求婚之後,才愛上了珍。我現在說的是個人的想法,你不一定要同意我。」艾瑪說。

「搞不好被你說中了。迪克森先生顯然是喜歡聽珍彈琴,而不喜歡聽她的朋友彈琴。」

P. 41

「而且他還救過她一命。你聽說過那件事嗎？他們搭船時發生意外，珍差一點掉下船，是迪克森先生抓住了她。」

「這我知道，我當時也在船上。」法蘭克‧邱吉爾說。

「真的？」

「真的。但事情發生得很快，我們都嚇了一大跳，所以看不出迪克森先生有特別震驚。」

「我本來是不確定，但是送來的這架鋼琴，證實了迪克森先生愛上珍了。」艾瑪說。

「我同意你的說法，那架鋼琴是愛的禮物。」法蘭克‧邱吉爾說。

第七章

P. 42

晚餐後，女士們先走向客廳，男士們不久也來和她們會合。

法蘭克‧邱吉爾先生走進去，他向貝茨小姐和她的姪女道過晚安後，逕自走向艾瑪坐的地方。她是他的目標，大家一定都看得出來。

法蘭克‧邱吉爾說：「我剛發現一件難過的事情，到明天我就已經在這裡待滿一個星期了——我停留的時間已經過了一半。」

「你現在大概很遺憾花了一整天的時間去剪頭髮。」

他笑著說：「不，我一點也不後悔。除非我看起來夠體面，不然就不喜歡和朋友見面。」

其他的男士現在都進了房間，所以艾瑪有幾分鐘得轉身背對法蘭克‧邱吉爾，聆聽柯爾先生說話。等柯爾先生走開時，艾瑪看到法蘭克‧邱吉爾正凝視著在房間另一邊的費法小姐。

「怎麼了？」艾瑪問。

他嚇了一跳，說道：「謝謝你叫了我，我剛剛很失禮，但實在是費法小姐弄了個很奇怪的髮型，我禁不住盯著她瞧。我一定要去問她那是不是愛爾蘭風格。我該去嗎？好，我要去。你可以看到她會怎麼接招——看她是不是會臉紅。」

P. 43

　　他立刻走了過去。很快地,艾瑪看到他站在費法小姐面前,和她聊了起來。只不過他站在她的正前方,結果艾瑪什麼也沒瞧著。

　　他還沒回來前,韋斯頓太太就坐上了他的椅子。

　　「親愛的艾瑪,我一直很想和你說話。你知道貝茨小姐和她的姪女怎麼來這裡的嗎?」

　　「她們當然是走過來的呀。」

　　「不,不是,她們是坐奈特利先生的馬車過來的。我想,他是為了她們才搭馬車來。」

　　「這很有可能,他慷慨又仁慈。」艾瑪說。

　　韋斯頓太太笑了笑,說道:「我想不只是慷慨喔。事實上,我才幫奈特利先生和珍·費法牽了線。你覺得怎麼樣?」

　　「奈特利先生和珍·費法!」艾瑪驚呼道:「親愛的韋斯頓太太,你怎麼會想得出這種事?奈特利先生不能結婚的,那我的外甥亨利怎麼辦?他要繼承奈特利先生的唐維爾寺院。」

　　「親愛的艾瑪,奈特利先生要是很想結婚,你總不能為了你六歲的外甥亨利,就阻攔他吧?」

P. 45

　　「我可以呀,我不能容忍亨利失去繼承權。奈特利先生去結婚,而且還是珍·費法,我想不出更妙的對象了!」

　　「他一直就最喜歡她了,這你心知肚明的。」

　　「他才不喜歡珍。親愛的韋斯頓太太,別開始幫人家配對,你的牽線很亂來。珍·費法成為唐維爾寺院的女主人!千萬不可以!奈特利先生不能做這麼愚蠢的事。」

　　「他是比她多金,年紀也有一點差距,可是我看不出有什麼不能匹配的。」

　　「可是奈特利先生不想結婚呀。他何必結婚?他自己一個人可逍遙了:他有農場,有羊群,有書房。而且他很喜歡他弟弟的小孩,他沒有必要為了填補時間或心靈,就去結婚。」

奈特利先生
- 艾瑪為什麼說奈特利先生沒有必要結婚?你覺得她說的對嗎?和夥伴討論。

P.46

「親愛的艾瑪，他要是真的愛珍・費法……」

「胡說！他才不愛珍・費法，我很確定沒這回事。」

「但我聽過他把珍講得捧上了天，他對她那麼感興趣，又那麼地擔心著她的健康！他那麼讚嘆她的鋼琴演奏和歌唱！我聽過他說，他可以一直永遠地聽下去。對了，我想，送給珍・費法鋼琴的人，搞不好是奈特利先生。」

「哦，我想不會，奈特利先生不會偷偷地做什麼事情。」艾瑪說。

「我確定是他送的。我有注意到，晚餐時，柯爾太太跟我們講鋼琴的事，他都沒吭聲。」

她們又聊了一會兒，直到柯爾先生走過來請伍德豪斯小姐彈鋼琴。她答應了。

接著，法蘭克・邱吉爾先過來唱歌，艾瑪便讓座給費法小姐，她的琴藝遠遠勝過艾瑪。

「我們在威茅斯合唱過一、兩次。」邱吉爾先生告訴賓客們。

P.47

艾瑪在離鋼琴不遠的地方坐下來聽。然後她注意到奈特利先生很仔細地聆聽，便又開始思索韋斯頓太太的猜疑。

她還是不希望奈特利先生結婚。「他的弟弟約翰・奈特利先生會很失望，父親也會很懷念奈特利先生每天都來訪，而我無法想像珍・費法去了唐維爾寺院，變成奈特利太太！不行，奈特利先生一定不可以結婚！」

奈特利先生走過來坐在艾瑪旁邊。剛開始，他們只談論這次的演唱。他稱讚珍的演奏，但沒特別的異狀。艾瑪說他很好心，送貝茨家的姨媽和姪女過來，但他不想聊這個，只因為他不想多講自己做的好事。

「坎貝爾家送的這架鋼琴，是很好的禮物。」艾瑪說。

「是呀。」他回答道，臉上並無窘色。「但他們為什麼不直說？出其不意是很蠢的做法。」

這下子艾瑪確定了，鋼琴不是奈特利先生送的。不過，他是不是墜入愛河了，她尚有懷疑。

P. 48

猜猜看

- 這架鋼琴是誰送的？
- 誰愛上了誰？如果你不知道，就繼續閱讀，找出答案。

珍的第二首歌快結束時，聲音有點沙啞了。

「這樣夠了，你一個晚上唱得夠多了。」奈特利先生自言自語道。

但很快又有人點了另一首歌，只聽到法蘭克·邱吉爾說：「我想這首歌對你來說是輕而易舉的。」

奈特利先生聽了火大，他說道：「那傢伙只是想炫耀自己的歌聲。」貝茨小姐這時正好從旁邊走過，他碰了她一下，說道：「貝茨小姐，你的姪女會唱把嗓子唱啞了，去叫他們別唱了吧。」

貝茨小姐於是不讓他們再唱下去。接著，有人提議跳舞。法蘭克·邱吉爾便走過來邀請艾瑪跳舞。

P. 51

在等候舞蹈開始之際，艾瑪張望著要看奈特利先生在做什麼。他是不太跳舞的人，而如果他這時候和珍·費法跳舞，就表示他對她有意思了。但是，他沒有，他在和柯爾太太閒聊。邀請珍跳舞的是別人。

艾瑪不再為小亨利操心了，他的繼承權穩當了。她享受這支舞，法蘭克·邱吉爾的舞跳得很好。只可惜，時間已晚，只夠跳兩支舞。

「這樣也好。」法蘭克·邱吉爾陪艾瑪

朝馬車走去，說道：「我不想邀費法小姐跳舞，你的舞藝比她好多了。」

第八章

P. 52

隔天還不到中午，法蘭克·邱吉爾就來到哈費。他走進房間，臉上堆著笑容。

「伍德豪斯小姐，我們要在皇冠客棧辦一場舞會。」他開口說道。

「皇冠客棧！」

「對呀，你一定要點頭才行。這是我父親的點子，韋斯頓太太也答應了。我把他們留在那裡，自己來哈費通知你。他們希望你去皇冠客棧和他們會合，他們想聽聽你的看法。」

艾瑪很開心，兩個年輕人便立即一起

123

動身前往皇冠客棧。韋斯頓夫婦看到她過來，很是高興。

他們一起逛了各個房間。在離開皇冠客棧之前，艾瑪答應前兩支舞要和法蘭克·邱吉爾一起共舞。等他們離開時，她聽到韋斯頓先生低聲對他的夫人說：「太好了，親愛的，他邀她共舞了。」

隔天早上，艾瑪坐著吃早餐，整個思緒想的都是舞會。早餐後不久，奈特利先生來訪。艾瑪跟他提到了舞會的事，但他興趣缺缺。

「為了幾小時吵吵鬧鬧的娛樂，這樣大費周章。當然，我是非去不可，但我寧可待在家裡。」他說。

P. 53

不過珍·費法很興奮，她說：「哦，伍德豪斯小姐，我希望不會有什麼意外讓舞會開不成，我真是期待。」

所以，如果不是為了要討好珍·費法，他是寧可待在家裡的。不是的！艾瑪很確定韋斯頓太太搞錯了，奈特利先生並不愛珍·費法。

令人難過的是，那天晚上邱吉爾先生寄來一封信，要法蘭克馬上趕回家，因為邱吉爾太太生病了。法蘭克得盡快啟程，前往安斯康柏。

韋斯頓太太寄了封短信給艾瑪，告訴她法蘭克·邱吉爾會來哈費和她道別。

舞會辦不成了，法蘭克·邱吉爾就要離開了，太慘了！

艾瑪已準備好，等著法蘭克·邱吉爾到來。

他到來之後，起初一會兒只是坐在那裡陷入沉思。

「這下子舞會辦不成了。」艾瑪說。

「如果我回來，我們還是可以辦舞會。還有，別忘了我們的舞。」法蘭克·邱吉爾說。

艾瑪笑了笑。

「我這兩個星期過得很愉快，真希望我可以待久一點。」他說。

P. 54

待久一點

▪ 你曾希望什麼時候能夠待久一點？勾選以下選項，和夥伴分享。
- □ 放假時　　　□ 上學時
- □ 派對時　　　□ 上數學課時
- □ 在朋友家時　□ 在床上時

「但你離開之前，不去拜訪友人、費法小姐和貝茨小姐嗎？」

「我已經去找過她們了。我路過她們的家，就覺得應該去拜訪一趟。」他猶豫了一下，站起身，朝窗邊走去。「伍德豪斯小姐，我想你可能已經猜到了，我……」

艾瑪感覺他快要說出她不想聽的事，便開口阻撓，說道：「我很高興你拜訪了費法小姐和貝茨小姐。」

他一語不發。艾瑪聽到他深呼吸了一口氣。她不希望他把話說出口，他也知道。「哦，老天！他對我的情意，比我想的還要濃。」她對自己說。

還好，這時她的父親走了進來，而法蘭克也該出發了。兩人親切地握了手，難過地說了聲再見，然後為法蘭克·邱吉爾關上門。

他離開了，艾瑪感到憂傷。她喜歡每天都能見到他。她想著：「這兩個星期過

得很有趣。他差一點就對我告白了。我現在悶悶不樂，我想我一定是有點愛上他了。」

第九章

P. 56

隔天，艾瑪與韋斯頓太太和奈特利先生喝茶時，聊到了珍·費法。

「但她為何想和艾爾頓先生與新婚妻子待在教區牧師的住宅？」艾瑪問。

「這樣比總是待在家裡好。」韋斯頓太太說。

「你說的對，韋斯頓太太。」奈特利先生說。

韋斯頓太太意有所指的看了艾瑪一眼。

沉默了幾分鐘後，奈特利先生說：「還有一件事——我確定艾爾頓太太不曾有過像珍·費法這樣的朋友。」

「我知道你很欣賞珍·費法。」艾瑪說。

「沒錯，大家都知道我很欣賞她。」他回答。

「不過你大概還不自知自己有多麼的欣賞她。」艾瑪說。

「哦！是嗎？但你知道得太晚了。柯爾先生六個星期前就問過我對珍·費法的感覺了。」奈特利先生說。

他頓住了。艾瑪不知道該做何感想。

P. 58

接著，他繼續說道：「不管怎麼說，我想珍·費法小姐不想嫁我，而且我也一定不可能跟她求婚。」

艾瑪聽了很高興，她嚷道：「你很謙虛，奈特利先生。」

他似乎沒有聽到她講的話，而是若有所思地說：「那麼，你覺得我該娶珍·費法嗎？」

「不，我不覺得。我不希望你娶珍·費法或是任何女孩。你要是結婚了，就不會陪我們坐在這裡閒聊了。」

奈特利先生又陷入沉思。他說：「不，艾瑪，我對她從沒動過

125

那樣的念頭。」過了一會兒，又説：「珍‧費法年輕可愛，但我覺得她太不坦誠了。」

聽到珍也有缺點，艾瑪感到開心。她説：「那我猜想你馬上就制止柯爾先生再多説了吧？」

「當然囉。我説他搞錯了，他跟我道歉，而且就不再説了。我並不是那樣子的。我是很欣賞珍‧費法，跟她聊天的感覺也都很好，但僅止於如此。」

等奈特利先生離開後，艾瑪説：「那麼，韋斯頓先生，你還覺得奈特利先生想娶珍嗎？」

「親愛的艾瑪，他一直説自己一定沒有愛上珍，我想到頭來他一定會愛上她。」

第十章

P. 59

一天早上，艾瑪陪著韋斯頓太太坐著，這時韋斯頓先生帶著一封信走來。那是法蘭克‧邱吉爾寄來的信。他即將再來海布里。

他們又開始著手準備皇冠客棧的舞會，大家都很興奮。再過不了幾天，海布里的年輕人就可以享受歡愉了。

終於，到了舞會之夜。法蘭克‧邱吉爾先生領著開心的艾瑪，走進舞池，跳了第一支舞。一想到接下來幾個鐘頭會玩得很愉快，她就很開心。然而，她卻起了煩惱，因為奈特利先生不跳舞。他應該跳舞的，而不是和那些為人丈夫、為人父親的人站在那裡！和那些上了年紀、挺著圓滾滾的肚子、身材短小的人

站在一起，他看起來又高又帥。大家一定也都這麼想！撇開法蘭克‧邱吉爾不説，他是舞廳裡最英俊的男人。

艾瑪

- 艾瑪為何開心？又為何生氣？想像你就是艾瑪，向夥伴説明你的感覺。

P. 60

大家繼續快樂地跳著舞，這時艾瑪突然注意到，奈特利先生正在和哈麗葉跳舞。艾瑪高興地想著：「正如我所料，他的舞跳得很出色。」

一直到晚餐過後，艾瑪才有機會和奈特利先生説話。而等他們重新回到舞廳後，他走過來和她交談。

他説：「親愛的艾瑪，你自認為很清楚法蘭克‧邱吉爾和費法小姐兩人的交情到什麼程度？」

「哦，是的，我很清楚。你問這個做什麼？」

「你沒想過法蘭克喜歡珍，或是珍喜歡法蘭克嗎？」

「沒想過！你怎麼會有這樣的想法？」她大聲説道。

「我最近看到他們之間有些心照不宣的跡象。」

「哦，那太好笑了！我敢打包票，他們之間沒有什麼。」

這時候，韋斯頓先生請大家再開始跳舞。「過來，伍德豪斯小姐、費法小姐，你們都在做什麼？過來跳舞吧。」

「我準備好了。」艾瑪説。

「你要和誰跳？」奈特利先生問。

她猶豫了一下，然後回答：「和你，如果你邀我的話。」

「我可以和你跳支舞嗎？」奈特利先生一邊伸出手，一邊說道。

「可以。」艾瑪快樂地說。

第十一章

P.63

隔天，他們一行人都去了伯斯山郊遊。這一天並不愉快，艾瑪一開始就覺得興味索然。「沒見過法蘭克·邱吉爾這麼悶、這麼無趣。」她心想。他兩眼視而不見，聽她說話卻不知她在說什麼。

等大家都坐下來，情況才好些，因為法蘭克·邱吉爾比較多話了，也會對艾瑪獻殷勤了。旁人看來，他們就像在打情罵俏。

P.64

艾瑪喜歡這樣受到矚目，但法蘭克沒有贏得她的芳心。實際上，她打算湊合他和好友哈麗葉。

艾瑪對法蘭克·邱吉爾說：「你把我說得太好了。」然後壓低聲音說：「但是，除了我們，大家都沒在說話，我們別淨說些廢話，為這七個沉默的人解悶。」

他說：「讓山上的大家都聽到我對你的讚美吧。」然後他低聲說：「我們要怎麼讓大家開金口？我知道了──各位女士先生，伍德豪斯小姐要我告訴大家，她想要每個人都說些有趣的事。她只有一個要求，要嘛來個巧妙的事，要嘛來兩個巧妙的事，再不然就來三件乏味的事，她保證聽了都會開懷大笑。」

P.65

貝茨小姐大聲說：「還好，那麼我就不用傷腦筋了。三件乏味的事，這個我做得到。」

艾瑪忍不住，她說：「啊，但這對你可能有點難，你只能說三件喔。」

貝茨小姐沒有立刻意會過來，等她聽懂意思後，很不高興。

「啊，我聽懂她的意思了。」接著她轉身向奈特利先生說：「我會盡量不要多嘴。」

韋斯頓先生大聲說：「我喜歡這個活動，我會盡力而為。來個謎語怎麼樣？」

「恐怕不太好。」他的兒子回答。

「哦，請說出來讓我聽聽。」艾瑪說。

韋斯頓先生說：「這雖然不是太巧妙，但是我要說了：所有的字母裡，哪兩個

字母代表完美？」

「我不知道。」艾瑪說。

「啊，你猜不到的，我確定一定猜不到。」他對艾瑪說：「我告訴你，是『M』和『A』——艾瑪。懂了吧？」

這並不有趣，可是艾瑪很喜歡，法蘭克·邱吉爾和哈麗葉也喜歡。其他人就不覺得有那麼好玩了。

P. 66

「這顯示了你們缺少了什麼樣的巧妙東西。韋斯頓先生表現出色，卻讓其他人都說不下去了，真不應該那麼快就到達完美的。」奈特利先生嚴肅地說。

「邱吉爾先生，可以的話，請跳過我們。」艾爾頓太太說。

「奧格斯塔，我們要去走走嗎？」艾爾頓先生說。

「好呀，請吧。在這一個地方坐這麼久了，我都膩了。來吧，珍，牽我的另一隻臂膀。」

珍沒答應，夫婦倆便走開了。

「真是一對佳偶！」法蘭克·邱吉爾說：「像他們這樣就結婚，真是幸運。他們當時在巴斯只相識幾個星期而已，真是好運！有多少人認識沒多久就結婚，然後抱恨終身！我希望有人會幫我挑選妻子。艾瑪，你要幫我挑選妻子嗎？只要是你挑選中的人，我一定喜歡。幫我挑個人吧，然後教導她。」

「把她教導得像我一樣。」

「如果你可以。」

「那好，我會的。你會有一個可愛的妻子。」

珍露出不悅的神情，她對姨媽說：「那麼，我們要和艾爾頓太太一起走嗎？」

「親愛的，如果你想的話。」她們起身走開，奈特利先生跟隨在後。

P. 67

只剩韋斯頓先生、他的兒子和哈麗葉留下來。法蘭克·邱吉爾愉悅的心情，簡直變得快惹人厭了，連艾瑪也對奉承和笑聲感到煩膩了。馬車來接他們回家時，艾瑪鬆了一口氣。

她在等候馬車時，奈特利先生走過來和她說話。

他說：「艾瑪，你怎麼可以對貝茨小姐那麼無禮？」

艾瑪想了想，臉紅了起來，想一笑置之。「她大概是沒聽出我的意思。」

「我跟你打包票，她有聽出來，她後來還說到這件事。艾瑪，你做得很不像話。這話是不中聽，艾瑪，但是我有機會就一定要跟你講，因為我是你的朋友。」

他們一邊談話，一邊朝馬車走去。馬車已經備妥，沒等她再開口說話，他就幫她扶上車。她什麼都沒說。她生自己的氣，而且覺得難堪。

上了馬車後，她靠著椅背坐了一會兒。之後，她想和他說聲再見，便轉過身看他，但已經遲了。他沒在看她，馬已經跑起來了。

P. 69

她怎麼會對貝茨小姐那麼殘忍！幾乎在回家的一整個路上，艾瑪感覺到眼淚撲簌簌地滾落臉頰。

艾瑪

- 你覺得艾瑪的行為不好嗎？
- 如果你的朋友對別人無禮，你會告訴他們嗎？
- 朋友應該對彼此說實話嗎？進行小組討論。

這趟糟透了的伯斯山之行，整晚都縈繞在艾瑪的腦際。她決定明天早上就去找貝茨小姐，跟她道歉。

艾瑪一回到哈費，就看到奈特利先生和哈麗葉正陪著父親坐著。

奈特利先生隨即起身，神情嚴肅，他說：「我離開之前，想見你一面。我要去倫敦，去陪約翰和伊莎貝拉幾天。你有要我帶什麼東西嗎？或是要我轉達什麼話嗎？」

「沒有。不過你這太突然了。」艾瑪回答。

「是沒錯。」

「他還沒原諒我。」艾瑪心想。

P. 70

奈特利先生準備辭行時，艾瑪的父親問：「我的老朋友（指貝茨太太）和她女兒如何呀？奈特利先生，親愛的艾瑪才剛去拜訪了貝茨太太和小姐。」

艾瑪的臉紅了起來，她看著奈特利先生。他對她笑了笑。

她很得意，而片刻之後，她更開心了。奈特利先生牽起她的手，就快要對著她的手親吻下去，但這時候，一個什麼原因，又讓他突然放手。

「他怎麼改變主意了？他不該停止的。」她心想。

之後，他旋即離開。

「真希望他不用那麼突然就離開。不過，我很高興他走的時候，我們還是好朋友。」艾瑪想。

隔天，一封信送到了藍道，宣布了邱吉爾太太的死訊。這件事令人難過又震驚。

129

「可憐的邱吉爾太太，她先前真的生病了！」

第十二章

P.72

大約在邱吉爾太太去世十天後的早上，艾瑪被叫到樓下去見韋斯頓先生。

他急著想和她說話，說道：「你今天早上可以來藍道嗎？韋斯頓太太要找你。」

「她不舒服嗎？」

「不是的，她只是有些不悅。你可以過來嗎？」

「當然。可是，是什麼事呢？」

「別問了，我答應太太不跟你說的。」

他們立即動身出發，很快便來到了藍道。

進入客廳時，他說：「好了，親愛的，我把她帶來了。」艾瑪聽見他低聲又說了句：「我有遵守承諾，她還不知情。」

韋斯頓太太看起來像是病了。

「怎麼回事？」艾瑪問。

「親愛的艾瑪，你猜不出來嗎？」韋斯頓太太用顫抖的聲音說道。

「我猜是和法蘭克·邱吉爾先生有關。」

「沒錯。他今天早上有過來，來找父親談話——他跟我們說，他戀愛了。」她停下來。艾瑪一開始以為說的是自己。

P.73

韋斯頓太太繼續說道：「他訂婚了，法蘭克·邱吉爾和費法小姐訂婚了。事實上，他們早就訂婚很久了！」

艾瑪吃驚得跳了起來，大叫說：「珍·費法！你不是說真的吧？」

韋斯頓太太回答說：「是真的，他們十月時在威茅斯就訂婚了。他們瞞著大家，沒有人知道這件事，他們騙過我們所有的人。他還這樣對你，我們無法原諒他。」

艾瑪沉思了一會兒，然後回答說：「我並沒有愛上他，你一定要相信我，韋斯頓太太，是真的。」

韋斯頓太太流著欣喜的眼淚親吻她，說道：「這下子韋斯頓先生放心了，我們一直為這件事情很苦惱。我們希望你們會看上彼此，而且還以為你們在談戀愛了。」

「我逃過了，我們都要很慶幸。不過，我無法原諒他，韋斯頓太太。他已經和別人訂婚，就沒有權利那樣和我打情罵俏。他當時怎麼知道我沒愛上他呢？」艾瑪說。

「親愛的艾瑪，從他所說的話聽起來，

我想……」

「她怎麼能忍受這種行為,看著他和別的女人當著她的面打情罵俏!」

P. 74

「艾瑪,他們兩個人之間有些誤會,他是這麼說的。他沒有時間解釋太多,他只來了十五分鐘。」韋斯頓太太繼續說道:「他很快就會寫信給我,我們等他來信,信裡頭大概就會解釋了。」

「邱吉爾先生怎麼說?」艾瑪問。

「他同意這件婚事。邱吉爾太太還活著時,這件事是沒指望的。法蘭克昨晚和邱吉爾先生談過,然後他今天一大早就離開。他先去海布里和珍碰面,然後就來到這裡。」

艾瑪說:「那麼,我祝他們幸福。」

珍和邱吉爾先生

- 你猜到了嗎?書上哪幾頁給了你線索?

第十三章

P. 75

當天稍晚,艾瑪期待著朋友哈麗葉來訪。

艾瑪心想:「可憐的哈麗葉,這下子不能嫁給法蘭克·邱吉爾了。」

「哦,伍德豪斯小姐!」哈麗葉快步走進房裡時,大聲說道:「我聽說了很奇怪的消息!」

「你是指什麼消息?」艾瑪回應。

「是珍·費法和法蘭克·邱吉爾先生的事,韋斯頓先生剛才告訴我的。」

哈麗葉看起來並沒有因為這件事而心情不好,她大聲說道:「你有想過他們是一對嗎?也許你早就知道,你可以看穿每個人的心思。」

「我開始覺得我沒有這種天賦了,我也是一個小時之前才知道。真是抱歉,哈麗葉。」艾瑪說。

「你幹嘛抱歉?」哈麗葉驚訝地喊道:「你該不會以為我喜歡法蘭克·邱吉爾吧?」

「你不久前才跟我說你喜歡他。」艾瑪回答。

「他?才沒有耶。」

P. 76

「但你說他對你很好,而且你對他也很有好感,我還說我並不意外。」

哈麗葉大叫:「哦,我的天呀,我現在想起來了,但我說的不是法蘭克·邱吉爾先生,不是!我說的是奈特利先生,舞會上沒人要和我跳舞時,只有他來邀我。我愛上的是奈特利先生。」

艾瑪很吃驚,「可是,你想奈特利先生對你有意思嗎?」

「有,我覺得有。」哈麗葉回答。

艾瑪靜靜地坐了一會兒。哈麗葉喜歡奈特利先生,這有什麼不好?然後她懂了,「我也喜歡奈特利先生!」

鬱悶的艾瑪聽著哈麗葉解釋。那場舞會之後,哈麗葉注意到,和以前比起來,奈特利先生更常找她講話,也對她更親切了!當大夥走在一起時,他常過來陪著她走,似乎是想瞭解她。

艾瑪知道確實是如此。哈麗葉轉述了他對她的讚美，艾瑪知道這也是真的。她內心很酸楚。

這時候，艾瑪的父親走進房間，兩人便沒再聊下去。

P. 77

白天剩下的時間，以及接下來的夜晚，艾瑪都心煩意亂。她要嘛動也不動地坐著，要嘛四處踱步；她試著待在自己的房間裡琢磨，或是待在花園裡琢磨。她想要弄明白、徹底地搞清楚自己的心意。

「我愛上奈特利先生多久了？他是何時取代了法蘭克‧邱吉爾？」她回想著，「我沒有喜歡過法蘭克‧邱吉爾！我喜歡的一直是奈特利先生。如果奈特利先生娶了哈麗葉，那是我咎由自取，是我給他們牽線。哦，拜託，別讓他結婚。如果他都不結婚，我就會很開心。」

艾瑪知道，就算奈特利先生跟她求婚，她也不能嫁給他。她不能拋下父親孤伶伶地一個人在哈費。

艾瑪和奈特利先生

- 你先前就猜到艾瑪愛的人是奈特利先生嗎？
- 書中哪幾頁給了你線索？
- 你覺得奈特利先生喜歡的人是誰？

第十四章

P. 78

隔天早上，哈費瀰漫著一股憂傷。到了下午，太陽露臉，艾瑪決定到戶外去。

她快步走進花園，讓她驚訝的是，她撞見了奈特利先生正穿過花園的大門，向她走過來。

「我一定要冷靜。」她告訴自己。

半分鐘後，他們會合了。兩人笨拙地打招呼，她問候他在倫敦的家人和朋友。大家都很好。他什麼時候離開他們的？就在今天早上。這趟旅程一定濕答答的吧？是呀。

他的神情和語氣不是很來勁。

「可能是因為他跟弟弟說他打算娶哈麗葉，結果弟弟反對了。」艾瑪心想。

他們一道走著。他不發一語，只是一直盯著她看。他大概是想跟她說他對哈麗葉的心意吧。她並不想要他這麼做，但她耐不住這樣的沉默，和他在一起，這樣很不自然。她想了一下，做了決定。她擠出笑容，開口說道：「我有個消息，會讓你嚇一跳。」

P. 80

「是嗎？什麼樣的消息？」他平靜地說道。

「哦，是天下最好的消息——一樁喜事。」

「如果你指的是費法小姐和法蘭克‧邱吉爾，那麼我已經聽說了。」

「怎麼可能？」艾瑪嚷道。

「韋斯頓先生今天早上寫信給我，他在信的結尾簡單地說了近況。」

「你大概不像我們其他人那麼驚訝，因為你起過疑心。我沒忘記，你提醒過我一次，但我沒聽進去。」

有一會兒，兩人都沒説話，接著她發現自己的手臂勾著他的，並貼在他的心口上。她聽見他説：「時間，最親愛的艾瑪，你終有一天會忘了他。」

他又挽住她的手臂説：「艾瑪，我感到難過。我很生他的氣。別擔心！他很快就要離開了。他們很快就會到約克夏。我為她感到惋惜，她可以找到更好的人才對。」

艾瑪明白了他的意思，她答道：「你人真好，不過你搞錯了。我沒有不高興，我只是為自己的行為感到羞愧而已。」

他大聲説：「艾瑪，就這樣而已嗎？」他停下來，「不，這我了解。請原諒我，你説得對，你會對他釋懷的！我原先不

確定你有多愛他，只是知道你喜歡他，而我覺得他配不上你。」

P. 81

「奈特利先生，我從沒有愛上過法蘭克·邱吉爾。」艾瑪説。

他一聲不響地聽著。她希望他説説話，但他沒吭聲。

她便繼續説道：「他是韋斯頓先生的兒子，經常來這裡。我一向覺得他很討人喜歡，而且，」她嘆一口氣：「他奉承我。但我從未愛上他。現在我懂了，他根本不想要我愛他。他和我打情罵俏，是為了掩飾他對珍的真正心意。」

説到這裡，她希望奈特利先生能有所回應，但他靜靜地沉思著。

終於，他開口了：「我一向不覺得法蘭克·邱吉爾有什麼好的，不過，看在珍的份上，我祝福他。」

「我確定他們在一起會很幸福的，我相信他們彼此很相愛。」艾瑪説。

P. 82

「他這個男人真有福氣！年紀那麼輕，才二十三歲，這種年紀來選妻子，通常下場悽慘。但法蘭克·邱吉爾很幸運，他在海邊遇見一個年輕女子，女子愛上了他，就算他和別人打情罵俏，也沒有讓她卻步。他的舅媽原本反對，但她過世了。他的舅父同意這門親事。他對每一個人都沒有分寸，大家卻都饒過了他。」奈特利先生説。

「你説得好像你很羨慕他。」

「我的確是羨慕他，艾瑪。」

艾瑪沒説話。她知道他在想著哈麗

葉，她不想聽到他說他喜歡哈麗葉，她不能讓他說出口。

接著，奈特利先生卻說了讓她詫異的話，他說：「你不問我羨慕什麼，你一點也不想知道，這很明智，但我就明智不了了。艾瑪，就算我等一下可能會後悔，我還是一定要跟你講。」

訴說

- 奈特利先生正想跟艾瑪講什麼事？
- 要訴說難以啟齒的事，你有過這樣的經驗嗎？

P. 84

「哦，那就別講吧，先想一想再說。」她喊道。

「謝謝你。」他尷尬地說，然後就沒再說話了。

艾瑪不忍心委屈他，他既然有話想對她說，她就應該聆聽。她可以幫他做決定，她可以說哈麗葉的好話。

這時，他們來到了房子前。

「你要進去嗎？」他問。

「不要，我們繼續走吧。」艾瑪回答。

走了幾步之後，她又說道：「奈特利先生，我剛才打斷了你，真是失禮。你如果想要聽聽我的什麼想法，身為朋友，是可以的。我會傾聽，並把我的想法據實以告。」

「身為朋友！」奈特利先生重複她的話。「艾瑪，我就怕這個字眼。不，我不想。等等，好吧，我為什麼要退卻？我已經說得很露骨了。艾瑪，我接受你的說法，以朋友的身分。那麼，告訴我，

你能愛我嗎？」

他停下腳步，凝視著她的雙眸。

他說：「我最親愛的艾瑪，不管我們這次談的結果如何，你將永遠是我最親愛、最摯愛的艾瑪，請立刻告訴我吧。你要是不得不拒絕，請直說吧。」

艾瑪說不出話，她欣喜不已。

P. 85

說話

- 你何時會說不出話？請打勾，並和夥伴進行問答。
  - ☐ 高興時。
  - ☐ 難過時。
  - ☐ 生氣時。
  - ☐ 尷尬時。

「我不會講天花亂墜的話，艾瑪。」他繼續說：「如果我喜歡你八分，或許我可以講到十分，但是你了解我的。最親愛

的艾瑪，你懂我的。」

他說話之際，艾瑪的腦子動個不停。她看到哈麗葉毫無立足之處，而她，艾瑪，才是他的全部。她不能要求他轉而去愛哈麗葉，或是跟他說自己又不愛他。

她說話了。她說了什麼？當然是該說的話，女孩總是這樣。她所說的話，足以讓他毋須絕望，也帶動他自己透露得更多。

P. 87

「我聽說法蘭克‧邱吉爾訂婚了，我很擔心你。聽到你根本沒有愛過法蘭克‧邱吉爾，這給了我希望，希望你終會愛上我。我從萬念俱灰，變成了幸福美滿。」

艾瑪也歷經同樣的轉變。在這半個鐘頭裡，兩人都知道彼此相愛著，也不再吃醋了。就他來說，他是嫉妒法蘭克‧邱吉爾的。

他說：「我對你的愛，和對法蘭克‧邱吉爾的嫉妒，是同時間開始的。我決定去倫敦，就是因為嫉妒法蘭克‧邱吉爾，我不想再看他和你打情罵俏。我離開，是為了想忘掉你。」他繼續說：「但是我去錯了地方。我弟弟的家庭太美滿，你的姐姐伊莎貝拉又和你太相像了。但我還是待在那裡，直到今天早上收到的信，講到了珍‧費法和法蘭克‧邱吉爾的事。於是，我待不住了，就騎馬冒雨回家，吃過午餐後，便直接步行來到哈費，就是為了要見你。然後，你告訴我，你沒有愛過他。」

幸福感又重返哈費。這時，兩個人正走回屋子裡，奈特利先生知道，她是他的親愛的艾瑪。

幸福

■對你而言，幸福是什麼？跟夥伴分享。

第十五章

P. 88

是時候了，艾瑪應該要跟父親說了！

「奈特利先生和我要結婚了，而且他會來哈費住。」她說。

父親一聽，起初大為震驚。

「爸爸，我不會離開哈費。我會留在這裡，而且奈特利先生在這裡，你會更快樂了。」艾瑪說。

「你這樣說是沒錯。」父親認同她的話。

這個消息讓大家都吃了一驚。大部份

的人都看好這一對，有些人覺得男方有福氣，有些人則覺得女方很好運。

一天晚上，艾瑪和父親造訪藍道。他們到達時，韋斯頓太太、法蘭克·邱吉爾和費法小姐都在客廳裡。

看到法蘭克·邱吉爾，艾瑪很開心，但兩人一開始有點尷尬。

法蘭克·邱吉爾走上前來，找她說話。「伍德豪斯小姐，謝謝你在寫給韋斯頓太太的信裡面，仁慈地原諒了我。」他說。

「恭喜你訂婚了。」艾瑪說。

P. 90

他又跟她道謝一次，然後望著珍，說道：「她看起來氣色不是很好吧？」他停頓了一下，接著問：「你難道沒有懷疑過珍和我嗎？」

「沒有，從來沒有。」艾瑪回答。

「這讓我很意外。有一次，我還差一點就對你全盤托出了。但願那時候我有講出來。」

「現在，這已經不重要了。你倒是要跟我說，那架鋼琴是你送給珍的嗎？」艾瑪說。

「對，是我。是我那天在倫敦買下的。」他笑著說

「沒有人猜到是你送的，我們甚至以為是奈特利先生送的！」

他說：「啊，奈特利先生還好吧？」他停頓了一下。

她一陣臉紅，笑了笑。

「恭喜你，聽到那個消息，我很高興。」法蘭克·邱吉爾說。

接著，他的心思又回到珍的身上，他說：「你看過那麼美麗的臉龐嗎？」

艾瑪回答：「我一直覺得她很美，但我記得你說她太蒼白了，你忘了嗎？」

他笑了笑。艾瑪說：「我覺得你喜歡捉弄我們所有人。」

「哦，不，我當時很難過的！」他說。

P. 91

艾瑪很開心能見到法蘭克·邱吉爾。不過，她當晚離開藍道時，她對奈特利先生的愛又更加深了。

那一年的十月，艾瑪和奈特利先生結婚了。參加婚禮的一小群友人所送上的祝福和願望，在他們幸福美滿的婚姻中，都一一成真了。

ANSWER KEY

Before Reading

Pages 8-9

1 a) F b) T c) F d) T e) T
2 b, c, e, f
4 a) 3 b) 1 c) 4 d) 2

Pages 10-11

5 a) 2 b) 3, 1, 4
   c) a: sitting
   b: dancing
   c: eating and talking
   d: talking and drinking
6 a) 4 b) 6 c) 3 d) 5 e) 1 f) 2
7 a) 4 b) 1 c) 5 d) 7 e) 6
   f) 10 g) 3 h) 2 i) 8 j) 9
8 a) embarrassed
   b) vain
   c) miserable
   d) kind
   e) nervous
   f) excited

Pages 12-13

10 a) excited
   b) vain
   c) kind
   d) miserable
   e) embarrassed
   f) nervous
11 a) 3 b) 5 c) 1 d) 2 e) 4 f) 6

Page 21

* Mr Weston's son by his first marriage.
* Mr and Mrs Churchill's nephew.

Page 32

* Jane.
* Very secretive.

Page 45

He's happy by himself.

Page 48

* Frank Churchill.
* Frank Churchill and Jane Fairfax are in
  love.

Page 59

* Mr Knightley is not in love with Jane.
  She is dancing with Frank Churchill.
* Mr Knightley should be dancing.

Page 82

* He is in love with her.

After Reading

Page 93

7 a) F b) T c) F d) T e) T f) F
8 a) 6 b) 5 c) 4 d) 1 e) 3 f) 8
g) 2 h) 7 i) 9 j) 10

Pages 94-95

10 a) 1 b) 1 c) 3 d) 2
11 kind, good-looking, thirty-seven, modest, generous
12 a) thirty-seven
b) good-looking
c) kind
d) generous
e) modest

Pages 96-97

13 a) father
b) neighbor
c) brother
d) sister
e) son
f) governess
g) wife
h) son
i) aunt
j) uncle
14 a) Mr Knightley
b) Mr Woodhouse
c) Emma
d) Frank Churchill
e) Jane Fairfax
f) Harriet

15 a) Jane Fairfax
b) Frank Churchill
c) Mr Dixon
d) Mr Knightley

Pages 98-99

18 a) flirted
b) flattered
c) was
d) in love with
e) criticized
f) fell in love
g) marry
h) got married to
19 a) ✗ Harriet is in love with Mr Knightley .
b) ✗ Mr Dixon is in love with Miss Campbell.
c) ✓
d) ✗ Frank Churchill is not in love with Emma.
e) ✓
f) ✓
g) ✗ Mr Knightley loves Emma.
20 No.

22

The story takes place in the little village of Highbury. The main character is Emma. Emma believes that she is very good at match-making. She enjoys imagining that people are in love with each other, but she is usually wrong. She is even wrong about herself.

One day, Frank Churchill, a very good-looking young man comes to stay with Emma's best friend, Mrs Weston. Frank is the son of Mr Weston, her husband. Emma imagines that everyone must want her to marry Frank Churchill. She herself thinks they are a good match. Sadly, she isn't in love with him. However, she believes that he is in love with her. They flirt together and everyone thinks that they are in love.

Later, they find out that Frank Churchill has tricked them all. He is secretly engaged to Jane Fairfax. He flirted with Emma to hide the fact that he is in love with Jane. When he announces his engagement to his father and Mrs Weston, they are very upset. They think the news will hurt Emma. Mr Knightley also thinks that Emma will be upset. By this time Emma knows that she is in love with Mr Knightley. Fortunately, he is in love with Emma. And so the story ends very happily with the marriage of Emma and Mr Knightley.

24 a) 3 b) 1 c) 4 d) 5 e) 2

25 a) shocked
b) vain
c) jealous
d) kind
e) miserable

27 a) 3 b) 5 c) 6 d) 4 e) 2 f) 1

28 a) was driven
b) were cooked
c) were looked after
d) were ironed
e) was taught

Test

1 a) 3 b) 2 c) 1 d) 1 e) 4 f) 3 g) 2

2 a) 19th century.
   b) Frank Churchill gives the piano to Jane Fairfax.
   c) She thinks Mr Knightley gives the piano to Jane.
   d) She thinks Mr Dixon gives the piano to Jane.
   e) Mr Dixon saves Jane.
   f) Everybody is excited about Frank Churchill's visit.
   g) Mrs Churchill is ill and she doesn't want him to go.
   h) She is his aunt. Her husband's sister is Frank's mother.
   i) M and A—Emma.
   j) She falls in love with him when he asks her to dance at the ball.
   k) They want him to marry Emma.
   l) He doesn't like weddings because they bring change.
   m) She realizes when he goes away to London.
   n) Yes, it does.

國家圖書館出版品預行編目資料

艾瑪 / Jane Austen 著 ; Elspeth Rawstron
改寫 ; 王傳明 譯. 一初版. 一[臺北市] : 寂天
文化, 2016.3 面 ; 公分. 中英對照

ISBN 978-986-318-436-2 (平裝附光碟片)

　　1. 英語　　2. 讀本

805.18　　　　　　　　　　105002697

原著 _ Jane Austen

改寫 _ Elspeth Rawstron

譯者 _ 王傳明

校對 _ 陳慧莉

製程管理 _ 洪巧玲

出版者 _ 寂天文化事業股份有限公司

電話 _ +886-2-2365-9739

傳真 _ +886-2-2365-9835

網址 _ www.icosmos.com.tw

讀者服務 _ onlineservice@icosmos.com.tw

出版日期 _ 2016年3月 初版一刷（250101）

郵撥帳號 _ 1998620-0 寂天文化事業股份有限公司